NOBODY LIVES FOREVER

Mark Preston reluctantly agreed to investigate the death of a junked-up kid who stole a car and killed himself joy-riding. Then wealthy Albert Augustin died and it was Preston who found the body. He also found Avis, the new widow who did her mourning in a bikini, and her body was by no means dead.

The key was the man named Nielsen, but the key was missing and Preston had to find it before too many people died—himself included.

NOBODY LIVES FOREVER

NOBODY LIVES FOREVER

by
Peter Chambers

c.1

MAGNA PRINT BOOKS
Long Preston, North Yorkshire,
England.

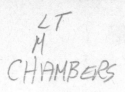

British Library Cataloguing in Publication Data.

Chambers, Peter *1924—*
   Nobody lives forever.
   I. Title
   823'.914 (F)

   ISBN 1-85057-620-3
   ISBN 1-85057-621-1 pbk

First Published in Great Britain by Robert Hale Ltd., 1964

Copyright © 1964 by Peter Chambers

Published in Large Print 1990 by arrangement with Peter Chambers, London

Printed and bound in Great Britain by
Redwood Press Limited, Melksham, Wiltshire.

CHAPTER 1

Outside, the night fog was chill. The City Publicity Bureau likes to talk about the occasional mists that rise in the evening, but this was no mist. This was fog, like a thick choking blanket. I sat in the office, wondering whether anybody else was working late. The desk lamp threw a bright circle of light on to the polished desk surface. Looking at that empty surface reminded me that I wasn't really working at all. Just sitting and waiting. The man who'd spoken to me on the telephone that afternoon was clear on two points only. He wanted to see me alone in the office at nine o'clock, and he wouldn't tell me who he was. For the third time in five minutes I checked the mechanism of the .38. Not that it made any sense. Anybody who wanted to do me any harm wouldn't go to the trouble of making an appointment to do it. I was making something of nothing. If you're going to attack somebody you retain the element of surprise if possible. You don't call him up and tip him off you're coming. I laughed at my own foolishness. Then

I checked the mechanism.

Out in the bay a ship's siren wailed sadly and I didn't blame it. This was no night to be out on the water. It was no night to be sitting in the office either, I reflected morosely. The sudden double tap at the door of the outer office almost made me jump out of my skin. The automatic jumped up from the desk and pointed towards the door, and I saw with surprise my hand was holding it.

'It's open,' I called.

The lights out there were on, and I'd left the connecting door open so I could see what was going on. A man stepped in, looked around expectantly, found the room empty. Then he saw me through the open door, and paled at the sight of the gun.

'C'mon in,' I invited.

He nodded as if to reassure me and kept his gaze riveted on the automatic all the way up to my desk.

'What's that for?'

He pointed. Before replying I had a good look at him. He was above average height, stockily built, and with stiff unruly black hair that sprang fiercely from the weatherbeaten forehead. Where I come from we're accustomed to plenty of tan, but this was not ordinary sun tan. This was weather. Wind and rain and sun had all made their contribution. This was an outdoor character.

'What it's for is to shoot with,' I told him. 'If you knew what a loveable personality I am you'd never believe this, but there are people who don't like me.'

He grunted and sat down. Nobody asked him, he just did it. If the gun bothered him he was keeping it well hidden from me.

'I don't like you or dislike you,' he informed me. 'I never even heard of you till today. All I know is you seem like a highly nervous character. Maybe I got a wrong number.'

'If you want to leave, the door is behind you,' I pointed out.

Truth was, the guy was making me feel slightly ridiculous.

'No offence,' he said. 'I guess you're in a funny kind of business.'

'Funny enough,' I agreed. 'I even get appointments with anonymous people late at night.'

He chuckled then, and waved a large hand.

'You got me. Guess it did sound kind of strange. Fact was, I wanted to be sure of two things. I didn't want you to go and tell anybody I was coming here.'

'And the other?'

'I wanted a little more time to check you out.

If I wasn't satisfied I just wouldn't come. That way you'd know nothing at all.'

'Which is about where I am right now,' I observed.

'Yeah. Say, will you please put that thing down?'

I laid the .38 on the desk, where I could get at it if I wanted.

'The name is Hawkins, Frank Hawkins. I'm second officer on the old *Star of Monkton.*'

'Ships are a little out of my line,' I said. 'What kind is she?'

'Freight mostly. We can take a few passengers, do some times. We ply between Monkton and Hong Kong, make a few stops to unload or pick up cargo. I just got back this morning.'

'Long trip?'

'The usual. Just over two months.'

A guy who's been at sea two months usually has one or two little things on his mind when he lands. It was the first time I'd heard of a visit to a private investigator figuring on the list.

'You haven't had much opportunity to get in the kind of trouble where you'd need me yet,' I commented.

He shook his head. The aggressive black hair danced around.

'This is not like that. It's about my brother Jeff.'

He paused and stared at his hands where they were clenched in his lap.

'Your brother is in some kind of trouble?' I prompted.

Slowly he wagged his head from side to side.

'He's all through with trouble. He's dead.'

There didn't seem to be anything I could say that might not be wrong, so I kept quiet.

'It was here in Monkton City,' he went on. 'Just a few days after I sailed.'

'What happened?'

'He shot himself full of junk, stole a car and drove it into a truck at eighty miles an hour. You must have read about it.'

I seemed to have a vague memory of the case, but it was just another of those wild kid deals, and I hadn't taken a lot of notice of it.

'Why have you come here, Mr Hawkins?'

'Because it stinks,' he replied simply. 'Jeff would never do those things. He was a quiet boy.'

That sounded too familiar. The weeping mother and the bewildered father explaining to the judge how Joey always helped around the house and went to church Sundays. Only Joey, in a moment of aberration, had stepped out of character long enough to rape the girl

11

across the street and stick a knife in her father when he tried to stop him.

'I don't remember much about the details, Mr Hawkins. Could you fill me in on those?'

'Well, as I told you, Jeff had injected himself with heroin. Then he stole this big Packard and went off and killed himself.'

'Yes,' I said patiently, 'But you're not satisfied it happened that way. You think there's something else.'

'I don't think it,' he replied emphatically. 'I know it. The hell of it is, I don't know what or why. That's why I'm here.'

'For me to find out?' I finished.

'Sure.'

I pushed my Old Favourites at him and we lit them.

'Anybody see this crash?' I asked.

'Plenty of people. It happened right outside the Beano Club just out of town. There was a party of people leaving to go on somewhere else. They all saw it. Eleven of them.'

'Any possibility that there could have been somebody else in the car with your brother? I mean, could somebody else have been driving and got away after the smash? It's been done before.'

'I thought of that one,' he said wearily. 'No chance at all.'

12

'Could the car have been started by somebody else and just pointed at the truck, with your brother too far gone to know what was happening?'

'No. It was going at a hell of a speed, the police worked it out at around eighty. In any case, Jeff had to drive around this wide curve just two or three seconds before he hit the truck. No, he was driving all right. The police went into all this kind of thinking. Man named Rourke, you know him?'

I knew a man named Rourke. Full name and title, Lieutenant John Rourke, Captain of Detectives, Homicide Bureau. It takes a tight-wad administration to call a man Captain of something and keep him on a lieutenant's pay, especially a man of Rourke's ability. If the hard-bitten Irishman had investigated the circumstances surrounding Jeff Hawkins death it would be no more than a waste of my time and his brother's money for me to try to come up with a different answer.

'Yes, I know Rourke,' I confirmed. 'Mr Hawkins, I don't want to be unsympathetic. I know how you must feel, and I can understand it. But Rourke is a very thorough officer, the best in the business. Believe me, if there had been one unsatisfactory feature of your brother's death Rourke would have hammered

13

at it until he had the answer. If he says that's what happened, that's what happened. And if he couldn't find anything suspicious about the crash, with all his resources, believe me I would have no chance at all.'

Hawkins sat and listened to this carefully. Then he nodded his head.

'I think you're right. I know one or two people in this town, and I asked about this policeman. They told me the same thing.'

'Then—?'

I shrugged my shoulders and looked at him enquiringly.

'Yes,' he said simply. 'Yes, I'm not doing so well at explaining, am I? I haven't been thinking too straight all day. This business about Jeff, it's put me a little off course.'

He sighed, and then, almost as though he were recovering from a punch, he shook his head quickly and blinked.

'Let me try again. I'm not saying the police were wrong. I'm not saying those witnesses made any mistake. That was my brother driving the car and he was doped when he did it. What I want to know is why.'

'Why?'

'Yes, why,' he repeated. 'You didn't know him and you don't know me, so I'll tell you a couple of facts. I've been around some, and

14

I've seen plenty. I know men and I know the dirty things they do. In my job you don't always see the pretty side of life. The man I knew better than anyone else was Jeff. And I'm telling you this was not him, not the real Jeff. So he stole a car, stuck a needle in his arm and went out and got himself killed. O.K that's what he did. But he didn't just decide overnight to go and act that way. Something made him do it, something we don't know about yet. Something means somebody. And, Preston, I want to know that somebody.'

He said it without inflection. He didn't wave his arms around or shout and stamp his feet. But I knew what he meant.

'And then you kill the somebody,' I finished.

He turned his head and stared at me dispassionately.

'That's hardly your business, is it?'

It might get to be my business, I thought. If Rourke thought I was using my curious talents to dig up murder-bait for revenge-seeking relatives, he'd think it was my business all right. Out loud I said,

'How old was Jeff?'

'Twenty-two,' he replied.

'And what work did he do?'

'He was trying to be a photographer but he hadn't made it yet. To fill his stomach he worked nights as a waiter.'

'Uh huh. Where?'

'Last time was a place called the Oyster's Cloister. You know it?'

'I know it.'

The place was run by a friend of mine I hadn't seen in a long time. Last time I was there he gave me some good advice* about minding my own business. Naturally I didn't take it. It looked as though I might be about due for another lesson.

'The photography,' I went on, 'That was what kind? Art stuff, newspaper shots or what?'

'Little of everything,' replied Hawkins. 'I think that was part of his trouble. He couldn't get it through his head you have to pick the thing you want and go for it. One week he'd be all rave about the on-the-spot picture of something happening, you know, the nose-for-news stuff. Then he'd see something in one of those expensive magazines he reads—I mean used to read—and he'd be off an artistic kick. You know the stuff, one drop of rain falling off a rose petal.'

I nodded.

'Was he any good?'

* The Big Goodbye.

16

'I thought so, but what do I know? With me, a camera is something for taking pictures of the family on vacation.'

'I'm with you there,' I agreed. 'Tell me more about him. Was he a serious man or high-spirited or what?'

'Serious mostly, especially about his photography. What was he like? Well, let's see. He was tall, well almost tall, about five ten and a half. Kind of skinny, but strong. That boy was strong as a horse. We used to wrestle some, and he'd give me a hard time now and then. I'm not exactly undersized.'

I looked again at the strong neck and thick muscled shoulders.

'He was strong,' I confirmed. 'Go on. Any love life?'

Hawkins looked slightly worried for a moment, then it was gone.

'Not that I know of. He'd been out with a few girls, naturally. But he wasn't the kind with a book of numbers. You could never imagine him just calling up some girl casually, and taking her out for the evening. With him everything had to be just so. He'd arrange a date days before, then spend hours getting ready for it. There'd always be flowers and candy, and he'd take her to the best place he could afford and give her the whole works. You

17

know, everything had to be just so. With Jeff a girl wasn't just a girl, she was something special. Maybe he was right for all I know. I went to sea at seventeen. You don't get to see too many of these pedestal-girls that way.'

'I guess not,' I agreed. 'Was there any special girl?'

He rubbed at his chin and there was a faint rasping from the emerging stubble.

'Funny you should ask that. I've been wondering about it myself. I had a feeling there might be these past few months. He would never tell me until he was ready, and I wouldn't ask, naturally. But I had this feeling maybe he'd found a girl who was taking her time about falling off the pedestal. Now I'm not so sure.'

'Why's that?'

'I'm his only relative in this city. If there'd been somebody Jeff was serious about, she'd have written me wouldn't she? Or come to see me or something?'

'Perhaps. But you've only been home one day. Besides, don't forget it's possible for your brother to have been serious about the girl, if there was a girl, without her being serious about him. For that matter, she might not have known anything about him. A serious kind of guy like that, he might have just admired her

18

from a distance. Somebody at the place he worked, or something of the kind.'

'Say, that is a possibility. I hadn't thought of that.'

Hawkins was talking more easily now, he was past the initial stiffness. I tried a question.

'Where did he live?'

'We have this apartment down off Oakhead. It isn't much, but it's kind of a home, or was. Why?'

'Did the police search the place?'

He looked puzzled.

'Why would they do that?'

'Whenever the police trace a narcotics addict —wait a minute, I know he wasn't but he seemed like one to them—they always search their homes to see if they can find any more of the stuff.'

'Oh,' he nodded. 'Well, they were in the place the day after it happened. The super told me that, but I didn't think about that kind of search. I imagined they only wanted to establish identity or something like that. With me being away and all. You think that's what they were after?'

I ground out my cigarette in the tray on the desk.

'I'm certain of it,' I told him. 'I also think they didn't find anything.'

19

'What makes you think that?'

'Because in addition to the decent news-papers in this city, we have a few garbage spreaders. If the law had turned up anything at your place, those boys would have found out and used it for extra smear when they reported the coroner's inquest. That's one reason. The other is that if anything like that had been found at your apartment, the narcotics boys would have been standing on the quayside to welcome you home today. And they would have turned you inside out. Don't forget it was your apartment just as much as his.'

'That's true.' He looked at me searchingly. 'Well, are you going to?'

I knew what he meant, but I didn't know whether I was quite ready to answer yet.

'Am I going to what?'

'Help me find out about the boy.'

I didn't know what to think. The family can never see any harm, not real harm, in their own people, but this Hawkins was making an impression on me. He wasn't a hysterical woman or a man who'd led a narrow sheltered life. Hawkins had seen the big world outside, and he didn't seem the kind who'd be easily deceived about his own brother. I thought he was heading for disillusion at best, bad trouble at worst.

'Let me ask you one,' I stalled. 'The boy was under the influence of drugs when he died. Now let's assume, and I am only assuming, that there is something to find out. Heroin is not something you pick up with the morning paper. You have to know where to go, and the people you get it from have to know you. The law is very tough on these people when it catches up with them. So they have to be careful nobody catches up. They'll go to a lot of trouble to see nobody does. They can play very rough if guys with long noses start pestering. You know what I'm talking about?'

He nodded.

'I can be rough if I have to be,' he asserted.

I contradicted him flatly.

'Oh no you can't, my friend. Not like these guys. They're not interested in standing toe to toe and slugging it out to see who falls down first. These guys like everything easy. Like four of them drag you out of bed in the middle of the night and work you over with brass knuckles and boots. Or if you can't take a hint a truck flattens you against a wall. You wouldn't have a chance, they never give anybody a chance. They're not in that line of business for emotional reasons but for money. If they have to look out for their interests they don't play Knights of the Round Table.

21

There's no percentage in it.'

He listened closely. Then he said,

'Why are you telling me all this?'

'Because I want you to have a clear idea of what you could be getting into. Once we start something we have to follow through. There won't be any chance to drop off between stations.'

He grinned quickly.

'Then you're in, huh?'

'I didn't say so,' I reminded him.

'Yes, you did. You said "once we start something". Not "once we started" or "if we started," but "once we start". So you've made up your mind.'

I had, at that. I thought it was a waste of time. I thought I was going to take Hawkins' hard-earned money for walking up a series of blind alleys and staring at a lot of stone walls.

'O.K.' I shrugged. 'I think you're wasting my time and your money. I'm expensive you know. And you'll get an account whether I dig anything up or not.'

'Don't worry about money.'

He got up, pulled a well-stuffed wallet from an inner pocket. From it he extended two bills and placed them on the desk in front of me.

'To get you started,' he announced. 'There's

more when you holler.'

Each bill was for one hundred dollars. I nodded.

'O.K. I'll get on it. Where do I reach you?'

'Don't try. I'll call here. If there's anything I ought to know leave a message with your secretary.'

'What's the mystery?' I asked suspiciously. 'I usually like to know where I find whoever's picking up the tab.'

'No mystery. Nobody knows I've been here, so there's nothing to connect you with me. I'm going to start asking questions myself. If there's anything phoney going on, people will expect me to be poking around. They'd think it was funny if I didn't. But you're different. Everybody knows who you are and what you do. If you start taking an interest, everybody will wonder why. You're the pro. And if it's clear you're not working for me, somebody might start to get afraid, might make a wrong move. That's when we make a score.'

It sounded all right, but I doubted whether it would work.

'It's kind of complicated thinking,' I observed. 'You're going to a lot of trouble to find something that probably isn't there.'

'It's there,' he stated. 'All we have to do is smell it out.'

I didn't contradict him any more. This was a man whose mind was made up.

'One thing,' I pointed out. 'You said if it's clear I'm not working for you. How do we make it clear?'

'It'll be clear,' he assured me. 'That's easy. I never saw you before.'

He turned around and walked through the connecting doorway. At the outer door, he turned again, flipped his hand to me and was gone.

I sat in the semi-darkness, leaning back from the bright ring of light. I dug out another cigarette, and watched the smoke curl luxuriously towards the edge of the light beam, where it seemed to linger briefly before sliding out into the safety of the surrounding gloom. With Hawkins gone, without his strong presence to influence me, I wondered why I'd let him talk me into the assignment. He admitted himself there was no doubt his young brother had done these things. All he wanted was to know why. Where would that get us? It could only mean more grief, not only for Hawkins, but maybe other people I hadn't even met yet. Anyhow, who said there had to be a why? People steal cars every day, especially young people. They don't call it stealing, they call it borrowing, joy-riding, anything but what it is. Plenty of

24

people got high on narcotics. They had fun-names for that too. Getting a lift, kicks, the big ball. These things are common, sad though it seems. The only thing different about the late Jeff Hawkins was, he had a big brother who wanted to know why. I sighed. If there was a reason, nobody was coming in to tell me about it. No mysterious visitor would materialise out of the fog for the sole purpose of wising me up about Jeff Hawkins. No. If there was a reason somebody would know it, somebody out there in the thick dank mist. The hundred-dollar bills stared at me reproachfully, reminding me they'd made the trip to my warm cosy of-fice for the express purpose of getting me out of it. Reluctantly I got up, scooped up the money and jammed it in a pocket. Then I pick-ed up the .38, patted it, and stuck it under my arm.

Outside, grey skinny fingers of fog scrabbled at the window, seeming to beckon me.

'O.K. O.K,' I grumbled sourly. 'I'm com-ing.'

CHAPTER 2

It was ten-fifteen when I parked outside the Oyster's Cloister. Or as near as I could guess was the outside. The lights across the sidewalk were vague through the mist blanket. I made it to the entrance and found the glass doors had been closed to keep out the fog. I pushed at the nearest door and it swung smoothly back to let me step gratefully into the well-carpeted hallway. The uniformed doorkeeper normally stood out front, but tonight he'd thought better of it, and I couldn't say I blamed him.

'Hello, Biff, how's business?' I greeted.

He blinked at me twice, Then,

'Mr Preston, ain't it? Nice to see you, Mr Preston. Business, it's busy. Can you tell me why anybody in his right mind wouldn't be in his own home if he could?'

'Search me,' I agreed.

I moved to one side as a beautiful blonde came storming for the door. Her features were too lovely to be screwed into that baleful expression. I didn't like to wince as I watched the mink in her swinging hand dragging along the floor. They say it's a sign of peasant blood if you worry about the cost of things. The peasant in me was having a ball as I watched that coat.

'Night, Mrs Van Dorn,' mumbled Biff.

'Julie.'

A man's urgent voice called, and a man in a white tuxedo hurried out of the entrance to the main bar.

'Julie baby, wait.'

Julie baby paused in the doorway, snorted impatiently and turned, just as he reached her.

'Hold this,' she snapped imperiously.

For some reason I held out my arms and several thousand dollars worth of fur dropped softly into them. Her right shoulder dropped and even then I didn't believe what I knew was going to happen. She brought her fist up almost from the ground. Tuxedo was about to say something, but he never finished it. She caught him right on the button. His mouth snapped shut and his whole head jerked back with the force of the blow. His eyes glazed over and he was out before he hit the floor. It was lucky the carpeting was so deep or he'd have cracked his skull.

The blonde snorted again, wheeled and stamped out into the fog. I looked down at the unconscious man on the floor.

27

'You think it'll fit you, Mr Preston?'

The grinning Biff pointed, and I realised the boxing blonde had left me with the coat.

'Hey. Mrs Van Dorn.'

I dashed outside and peered vainly into the gloom. A car motor whirred impatiently, then suddenly roared into life. Thoughtfully, I made my way back inside.

'Mrs Van Dorn seems to have gone, Biff.'

'Yeah,' he agreed. 'Well, I better clean up this mess here.'

'Mr Van Dorn?' I queried.

'Nah,' scoffed the other. 'He died a coupla years ago. I don't know this guy at all. Want me to take care of the coat?'

I began to hold it out, then changed my mind.

'No, thanks, I'll see she gets it.'

'If you say so, Mr Preston.'

He bent down and hooked his elbows under the armpits of the loser.

'Boss in?' I asked.

'Sure—He's in the office.'

I thanked him and went along the hall to the door marked 'Manager'. I tapped twice and opened it.

Reuben Krantz was sitting at a table by the wall. In front of him the glow of the deep-polished surface set off the rich gleam of silver table-ware. He was raising the cover of a steaming dish as I closed the door.

'Well, well, the great detective. How are things, Preston?'

'Not bad, Ben. You?'

'I make a living' he admitted. 'Is it that cold?'

He pointed a heavy knife towards the mink.

'It isn't mine,' I replied. 'This one is too tight across the shoulders.'

I told him what had happened outside. He tutted.

'That is a high-spirited dame, that Van Dorn. Man, if I had a string of horses with her fire I'd clean up. You leaving the coat with me?'

'If you say so,' I replied. 'I was sort of hoping you wouldn't mind if I returned it to her personally. She's quite a girl.'

'Take it, take it. I have five dollars says you won't last three rounds with her.'

'Done.'

I pulled up a chair and sat close to the table. Krantz said,

'This is my eating time. You hungry?'

'Not right now.'

'Well, go ahead and talk. I'll eat if you don't mind.'

He helped himself from the dish. In the

Oyster's Cloister they had a reputation for fine food for twenty miles around. There was no delicacy so unusual you couldn't get it at the Cloister. The French chef, Armand, was not the routine Armand from Arkansas. This particular Frenchman was from Paris, France, and there were many wild estimates of just how much Krantz had had to shell out to prise Armand out of one of the leading Paris hotels. With that kind of cuisine, you'd expect the guy who owned the place to have something special in the way of an evening meal. Krantz did indeed have something special. A brew of pigs knuckles cooked specially for him every night in the delicatessen across the street. Krantz wanted knuckles, Armand wouldn't serve knuckles, so Krantz had to import his food.

I let him have the first few mouthfuls in peace. Then I said,

'I hear you lost a waiter, Ben.'

He frowned, stopped chewing, then shook his head.

'Wrong number,' he contradicted. 'Nobody quit in weeks.'

'This was weeks ago I'm talking about. Nearly two months. Kid named Jeff Hawkins.'

Another frown, not puzzlement this time, but concern.

'I remember that one. Maybe it'll begin to

make sense now.'

It was my turn to look puzzled.

'Huh? I don't follow that.'

He wiped a snowy napkin across his lips, reached for the schooner of beer in his hand, and took a deep draught.

'Warm,' he grumbled. 'You'd think in my own joint I could get a cold beer when I want it.'

'What'll make sense now?' I persisted.

'You coming here. I couldn't figure the Hawkins kid taking off that way. Did you know him?'

'Uh uh.'

'I knew him a little bit. Took him on here myself. Nice kid. Quiet, well-behaved kind. Kind you'd want your own boy to be, you know? Quiet dresser, knew how to speak to people, all kinds of people. Smart, too. He'd never worked in a place like this before, but inside a coupla days you'd think he grew up in the business. So why would a boy like that go get himself killed that crazy way? I tell you, Preston, it worried me. Didn't make any kind of sense at all.'

'So what difference do I make?' I wanted to know.

'Obvious,' he waved a napkin at me. 'You're asking questions about him, or you're going to.

31

You're a private investigator, very expensive they tell me. So everybody said he was just another hipped up kid, and it was a good job he got killed before he killed somebody else. People who knew him, knew it had to be something else, something that didn't come out. Now from thin air there's you. So there was something. You either know it already or you're going to find out. That's what I meant when I said it begins to make sense. Your turn.'

He returned to the attack on the knuckles. They smelled very good to eat and I made myself stop staring at them with my starving python look.

'I don't know whether there's anything in this or not,' I hedged. 'Just asking around, usual thing. Try to get a few facts and a whole lot of opinions.'

Krantz nodded.

'S' O.K.' he assured me. 'You always did keep 'em close to the table. I don't mind. Go ahead, ask me something.'

I asked him for anything he cared to tell me about Jeff Hawkins. Habits, likes and dislikes, who were his friends. Krantz couldn't tell me much that was of real value. After all, the boy had been only one of thirty or more people who made up the payroll at the Cloister. Krantz was

32

not the man to interfere with their affairs unless someone started getting too far out of line.

'I'm not much help, huh?' he sighed. 'Talk to Ernie, my captain out there. He liked the boy.'

I got up to leave, draping the mink over my arm.

'Thanks, Ben, I will. Here.'

I went to the ornate desk, took a jar of bicarb and a spoon from the drawer and placed them where he could reach them. After the knuckles and the beer, Krantz's stomach would present its own kind of check, a pain that always bent him double. Now he grinned.

'It'll save you crawling over there in agony ten minutes from now,' I told him.

'Thanks,' he grunted. 'Don't forget to return the lady's coat. I'd be upset if I thought she wasn't going to get it back.'

'My, my,' I murmured. 'So the pains have started already, huh?'

As I closed the door, his face was buried in the foaming beer again.

Biff was back at the same old stand by the door.

'What happened to the guy with the glass jaw?' I demanded.

'I called a cab and sent him home,' he replied. 'You want a cab, Mr Preston?'

'No, thanks, my car's outside. What's a good time for me to talk to Ernie?'

He looked at the wall-clock. It was ten forty-five.

' 'Bout an hour, I guess. He usually takes a break just before midnight for about twenty minutes.'

'That should give me time to return the lady's property,' I decided. 'What's the address, Biff?'

His face went blank.

'I wouldn't know, Mr Preston. Don't take that much interest in the customers. Guess you might find it in the book, though.'

'Uh huh. And I might not.'

I took two fives from my pocket and tucked them under one of the gold shoulder flashes.

'I didn't bring my reading glasses,' I told him. 'You look it up for me, huh, Biff?'

He shook his head.

'Wouldn't do any good, Mr Preston. She isn't in there. But I just remembered where she lives. 1616 Alohah Apartments. She's always leaving things around. I had to go there coupla weeks back. She left a purse here, nearly eight hundred bucks inside.'

'So glad you were able to recall it,' I said. 'See you later.'

After the warmth of the interior the night air,

with its rich fog additive, struck chill against me. I hurried across the sidewalk, tossed the coat on the back seat of the Chev, climbed in and gunned the motor. Then I eased gently away from the kerb.

CHAPTER 3

The Alohah Apartments were about as high-priced as you can get. When people talk about prices they talk in ranges, like medium-price range, high-price range. With the Alohah, ranges were out. This was the summit price. I'd only ever been inside once before. That was to persuade an errant teen-age girl that the seventy-year-old goat who was feeding her champagne didn't look on her as a daughter at all. It was only when I told her it was the guy's granddaughter who'd hired me, that I persuaded her to leave. The little scene had attracted attention from one or two of the other tenants, and I hoped none of them would re-member me tonight.

The concrete and glass cliff towered above me and disappeared quickly into fog as I walk-ed from the car to the entrance. A thousand separate existences were going on right that moment behind the impassive smoothness of the walls. Most of them I'd never hear or know about. There was one though, a certain lady in 1616, about whom I'd like to know more. The elevator sped with silent smoothness to sixteen. I got out, still toting my spare skin, and poked around the quiet corridors till I found the number I was looking for. I pressed gently at the bell and waited. After a moment the door opened and a pretty coloured girl stood looking at me.

'Mrs Van Dorn?' I asked.

She paused uncertainly.

'I don't know. It's awfully late. Who's calling, please?'

'Tell her my name is Mark Preston. I'm a hunter. Look what I caught.'

She saw the coat now.

'Oh. Oh dear. Just a moment, please.'

Evidently I wasn't going to steal anything, because she didn't close the door. Within seconds she was back.

'Will you come in, Mr Preston?'

I would come in. I stepped into the quiet luxury that goes with the rental in a place like the Alohah.

'In here, please.'

She opened a door for me to go through, and closed it behind me.

Julie Van Dorn was sitting by a record player listening to the music. I didn't know the track but I knew the title would be something like Lovesongs for Lazy Lechers. It was one of those long-playing deals with thousands of violins softly suggesting discreet lighting, cold champagne and everything that goes with it. What went with it was Julie Van Dorn and I kept right on looking at her.

She was wearing a dark green blouse tucked into cerise ballet tights. The shining gold of her hair tumbled round her cheeks as she sat, head in hands, dreaming to the music.

'Ah,' she said brightly. 'The hunter.'

'Thought you might need this. It gets cold these nights.'

I put the coat down on a chair.

'Thanks,' she said carelessly. 'What'd you say your name was?'

'Mark Preston.'

'I'm Julie Van Dorn.'

'I know. That's why I'm here.'

'Oh?'

For the first time she showed some interest in me.

'What does that mean exactly, Mr Preston?'

'It means you're a beautiful girl, and what better excuse could I ever have for talking to you?'

'So talk to me. I'm bored to death anyway. Come and sit for a minute.'

I perched opposite her. She looked at me appraisingly with soft grey eyes.

'You have a good body,' she remarked casually. 'You oughtn't to let it run to seed like that.'

Without realising it I pulled my shoulders back and stuck out my chest.

'No good doing that just because you remembered suddenly. It ought to be that way the whole time,' she censured. 'Smoke?'

'Thanks.' I looked around for cigarettes.

She shook her head impatiently.

'I wasn't asking whether you wanted one, but whether you smoked. Anyway it's answered. I could tell you did. Drink too, I'll bet.'

'I drink if I want to,' I acknowledged. 'You seem to have a physical culture thing.'

She smiled fleetingly.

'Not so much these days. When my father was alive, what you just said would have been the understatement of the year.'

I must have looked puzzled at that because she went on at once.

'He was a fighter, my father. Do you follow the fights?'

'A little. Would I have heard of him?'

'Perhaps. They used to bill him as the Murderous Mick. He got as far as challenging the title holder once in the light-heavy division.'

'It was a little before my time,' I remarked. 'Would have been over twenty years ago, wouldn't it? I've certainly heard the name before.'

'Yes,' she nodded. 'He stopped fighting when I was a small child. But he didn't believe in running to seed. He hadn't a son, just the two girls, my sister and I. While all the other girls were playing with dolls we were doing physical jerks. He even taught us to fight.'

'So I noticed back at the Cloister,' I said. 'I knew you didn't pick up that footwork at a ladies' finishing school.'

The music had finished and with a soft click the record-player switched off. She sighed.

'Well, that's enough about me for now. How about you, Mr Preston. You do anything else but hunt mink?'

'I'm a private investigator,' I told her and watched for her reaction.

When people hear me say this, they react in many different ways. Some look guilty as though wondering whether I can possibly know about that weekend in Pasadena. Others look furtive as though hoping nobody sees them talking to anybody like me. Some are interested and want to hear about it. There are some, bless'm, who smile politely and obviously haven't the vaguest idea what I'm talking about. Julie Van Dorn said,

'Does it keep you busy?'

'Busy enough, I can always find time to run an errand like this one.'

She misunderstood that.

'Oh, why of course, I haven't said anything about a reward have I? What would be fair for returning a coat like that? A hundred dollars?'

I sighed.

'You missed the point, Mrs Van Dorn. What I meant was, I can always find time to do a favour for a beautiful girl. And I don't need a hundred dollars.'

She flushed slightly.

'I'm sorry. And as far as my being beautiful goes, you can forget it. I'm all through with the male of the species in any romantic way.'

'It seems a pity,' I observed. 'Was that why you socked that character tonight?'

'Howard? He was being a bore. There are only two kinds of men. I've decided. One half are only interested in getting me into bed, and the other are working out exactly how to get hold of some of my money.'

'You're being unrealistic,' I told her. 'That's the way the world is for everybody. The romance bit and the profit motive. Just to keep the records straight, let me say I'm not interested in your money.'

'Just to keep the records straight,' she mimicked, 'let me say what you're interested in is of no concern to me whatever. You returned my coat, and thanks. You don't want a reward, that's up to you. Thanks again and goodnight.'

I was being thrown out, and it nettled me. Perhaps I'd used the wrong approach. At the door I turned and said,

'You're way out of shape with your ringcraft. Just because you slugged some barfly when he wasn't looking, don't get the idea you're any kind of female Joe Louis.'

She was quickly interested. With some annoyance she snapped.

'You think you'd do any better than he did?'

I laughed derisively.

'Try me sometime.'

'I'll try you now.'

She said it softly, almost with a hiss. Uncurling herself from the chair she stood upright and came across to me. Her attitude was one of tense threat, the way I'd seen her earlier at the Cloister. I tried to look worried.

'Look,' I muttered. 'This has gone far enough. I can't fight a woman.'

'We'll know soon enough,' she replied.

Almost imperceptibly she moved her weight on to the balls of her feet. Her left shoulder came forward as the right hand began to move,. At the last second I swung my left hand to ward off the hook and at the same time slapped her lightly across the face. She shook her head in astonished fury and swung again. This time I let it come, ducked underneath and came up behind her as the force of the blow swung her round. Grabbing her right wrist I brought her arm sharply down and bent it up behind her back.

She said a word she hadn't any business to know, and I stepped round her left side, keeping hold of her right hand and pinning her left as I came. She glared into my face and I smiled at her.

'You want to stick to the drunks,' I advised.

My right arm was almost encircling her now. She struggled furiously to free her hands and I waited for the fuss to die down. She was strong and I had difficulty in holding her with one hand, but I didn't want to give her the satisfaction of seeing that I needed both to keep her quiet. With my free hand I grabbed her under the chin and lifted her face, not too gently.

'About that reward,' I grinned.

I kissed her hard and kept on doing it. She made no response at all, other than to struggle even harder than before. But there was nothing she could do to stop me, and I wanted her to know this before I freed her mouth. She didn't melt in my arms the way women are popularly supposed to under such circumstances. She just stood there radiating silent fury. When I lifted my head though, I was surprised to see her eyes were closed.

'Are you all through?' she said coldly.

'I think so. If I let you go, will you start swinging again? I warn you I won't be so gentle next time.'

'All I want is for you to get out.'

I let her go and stepped away. She stood quite still, not looking at me. I wished I could read her mind at that moment.

'Goodnight, Mrs Van Dorn.'

She ignored me as I went out of the room. The maid appeared from nowhere to open the outer door.

'Goodnight, Mr Preston.'

'Goodnight, honey.'

It was time for me to get back to Krantz's place.

CHAPTER 4

Biff told me I'd find Ernie in the band-room at the rear. I looked round the door and saw a spare little man about fifty years old sitting reading a late paper. By his hand was a plate of sandwiches and a cup of coffee.

'Are you Ernie?' I asked.

He looked up, no emotion showing on the well-trained features.

'Mr Preston? Mr Krantz told me you might look me up.'

I closed the door and sat down near him.

'Sorry to bust into your break this way. I'll be as quick as I can. I'm interested in what happened to Jeff Hawkins. Anything you can tell me will help.'

'What kind of anything?'

He selected a thin sandwich from the pile and began to munch on it.

'To begin with, did he ever strike you as somebody who'd do anything wild?'

'Wild? Uh huh. Not Jeff. Never.'

Ernie leaned forward in his chair.

'I've got a theory about that business, Mr

Preston. I never mentioned it to a soul till now, except my wife that is. But Mr Krantz told me who you are, so I guess I can tell you.'

'Go ahead, I'm interested.'

'Well,' he looked quickly around the small room as though to be certain we were alone. 'It's like this. I have three daughters, Mr Preston. Beautiful girls, good girls. And I tell you this, with no reservations. If Jeff Hawkins had come around courting one of my own girls, I would have been proud and pleased. Proud and pleased. That'll give you an idea what I thought of the boy. For him to do a thing like that was impossible. But he did it, he did it. So we have to wonder exactly why he did it. Now I'm gonna tell you what I think.'

He swallowed the last of the sandwich, wiped his mouth carefully on a spotless napkin and laid it on the table.

'He was running away, that boy. From gangsters.'

He said the word in a whisper, as though there might be a dozen hoods waiting in the passage outside.

'Gangsters?' I queried. 'I wouldn't have thought he'd know too many of those, a quiet fellow like that.'

He wagged a finger knowingly.

45

'No, and you'd be right. But suppose he heard something, about a big robbery or something of the kind. You'd be surprised at some of the things a waiter hears in a place like this. Now, suppose these men realised Jeff knew something. They kidnapped him, filled him full of this—this—'

'Heroin,' I supplied.

'Sure. Filled him with this stuff to keep him quiet. Somehow he broke out of wherever he was, grabbed the first car he could see and drove away as fast as he could. He didn't realise how much the drug was affecting his judgment and he went slap into that truck and killed himself.'

It was an ingenious idea. I pondered on it.

'You haven't been to the police with this theory?'

Ernie shrugged.

'I thought about it, naturally. Then I thought, what good would it do. It wouldn't change the facts, would it? If it had been a question of catching a murderer, I would have gone to them straight away. But the sad truth is, the boy killed himself, although he didn't mean to. The police could never find out whatever it was he'd discovered, because he was the only one who knew and he was dead. They'd only be working in total darkness and they

46

couldn't possibly get anywhere. So, as I say, it wouldn't do any good. On the other hand, if these people, these gangsters, found out I'd suggested such a thing to the police, they'd have to do something about me.'

'Why?' I asked.

'Because the boy worked under me. We were kind of friends in a way. They'd never be sure he hadn't passed on to me whatever it was he'd found out. They might come for me, Mr Preston, I'm not a brave man. I couldn't take that kind of thing.'

He said it half-sadly, half-apologetically. I tried to cheer him up.

'There could be something to your theory. I'll certainly bear it in mind. Tell me about his other friends. Was there a girl?'

He nodded.

'Oh yes. He never talked to me about her, but I've seen them together. Pretty little thing, not much more than twenty years old. Name of Sue, I don't know the last name.'

'Know where she lives?'

'No.'

Then seeing my disappointment he added hastily,

'But I know the place she works. There's a delicatessen across the street. Miller's. That's where she works.'

And that was how Jeff Hawkins came to meet her, I reflected. Miller's was the place that prepared Krantz's nightly intake of pigs knuckles. Jeff had probably been sent over to pick up the tray, and there was Sue.

'I heard there was a brother, too. That right?'

He nodded vigorously.

'Oh, yes. He was a sailor of some kind, an officer, I think. Jeff thought a lot of his brother, looked up to him. They used to share a place, that is when the brother was home. You ought to see him really. He's the one can tell you about Jeff.'

'When he gets back from his trip I'll look him up,' I agreed. 'Did Jeff ever talk about his photography to you?'

'No. I knew he was interested in it, but I couldn't talk to him. I always say if you don't know anything about a subject, best thing is to keep quiet about it. About photography I keep very quiet indeed.'

He chuckled at his little joke, and I smiled too. I liked the little guy, he was like some terrier dog who was anxious to please everybody.

'Well, I've taken up enough of your time.'

I got up and shook hands with him.

'Thanks a lot, Ernie. If you think of anything, anything at all that might help me, ring this number, will you?'

He took the card, and promised that he would.

'Sorry I wasn't more help,' he apologised.

'Everything's a help,' I reassured him, and went out.

It was five minutes after midnight. I went past the bars on my way back to the entrance hall. When I was almost at the door it was pushed open and three men walked in, talking noisily. Two were strangers, but the third one was Frank Hawkins. He saw me at once, stared stonily over my shoulder and walked on past. I went up to Biff, the doorkeeper.

'Never see a familiar face these days,' I complained.

'Them? Oh they're pretty regular lately, Mr Preston. You ought to get out more.'

'I guess that's right. Thought I knew that last one, though. Isn't he a fighter or something?'

He shrugged.

'Could be, I never saw him before.'

'I thought you said they were regulars?' I queried.

'The other two, yes. Them I know. They're in the hardware business. The Elman brothers. The one with the glasses, that's Georgie Elman. The other one's his brother Cy. That last guy, he coulda been a fighter at that. Had that kind of look about him.'

'I'm probably kidding myself, Biff. Just desperate to recognise somebody I guess.'

He hadn't any comment to offer on that, and I went back out into the fog. I drove to the nearest pay-phone and called Joe Carpenter. Joe is a very useful character to know, especially when you're in my line of business. He has access to all kinds of information that might take anybody else days or even weeks to acquire. The bell jangled for three or four minutes, then an irritable voice said,

'What is it?'

'Joe?'

There was a pause.

'Look, you woke me up, whoever you are. I don't have to be dragged out of bed just to find out who I am. Now just tell me who you are and what you want.'

Even for Carpenter, it was obvious he was unusually peevish.

'This is Preston, Joe. Look, I'm sorry to bother you this late—'

'—sorry you should be—' he grumbled.

'—but I want to check a credit rating.'

'What?'

I thought he was going to jump into the receiver and come rushing out at my end. He gave me a minute or so of his time. It was devoted to private investigators in general, one Preston in particular, and was liberally sprinkled with heated references to the time of night and the merits of the credit rating system. I waited while he talked it out.

'I have all that, Joe, and thanks for your views. Now, about this information I want, do I get it?'

He simmered down.

'Depends on who it is,' he snapped. 'I don't carry a card reference system home to bed with me, you know.'

'Sure, Joe, naturally. But these are business guys, so maybe you'll know off the cuff.'

'What business?'

'Hardware. The Elman brothers, Georgie and Cy. Ring any bells?'

He chuckled. It was his first human sound since picking up the telephone.

'Credit rating? The Elmans? You must be kidding. Any credit rating those guys have wouldn't get you enough free ice-cream to put on a fly's tail.'

'Not a very reliable business, huh?' I ventured.

'I can't discuss the details over the phone. Tell you what, if you really want the inside on those guys you have the wrong number. You know Vince Brooks?'

'Sergeant Brooks of the Fraud Squad, you mean?'

'That's the one. Ask him about their credit rating. Only take my advice, don't call him up in the middle of the night. He doesn't have my forgiving nature.'

I thanked him and hung up. After searching my pockets for more change, I dialled another number.

'Police Headquarters,' said a crisp voice.

'Who has the duty in Homicide tonight?' I asked.

'What is this, Information Please? Who's that calling?'

I told him.

'Wait a minute, I'll ask the desk sergeant.'

After a few moments he came back on the line.

'You still there? It's Lieutenant Rourke, and he's in.'

'Thanks. I'll come over and see him.'

'Suit yourself.'

He didn't sound very encouraging, and I could understand it. Rourke's right hand was a certain sergeant by the name of Randall and Randall had contracted the mumps, of all things. The police department of our fair city is always overworked and undermanned. Rourke's temper at the best of times is inclined to be somewhat uncertain. Deprived of the valuable services of Randall he would be like a bear with a sore head. But he was the only one who could tell me what I wanted to know. I climbed into the Chev and inched my careful way across town to headquarters.

CHAPTER 5

The desk sergeant knew me. He looked up and made a face as I approached.

'You must be hard of hearing,' he greeted. 'I told them to tell you Rourke was here.'

'They told me,' I confirmed. 'I want to see him.'

'Did you know Randall was off duty, sick?'

'Yeah.'

'And you still want to see the lieutenant,' he marvelled.

'Some of you guys don't know when it's time to go home.'

'Thanks for the encouragement. Can I go up?'

He waved his pen.

'Go up, go up. If I were you, I'd go up slow. No telling how fast you're liable to be coming down.'

I trudged up the badly lit stairs. Some day an ex-cop is going to be made mayor of our fair city, and when that happens the taxpayers are due for a shock. The ex-cop mayor is going to demand several million dollars for the purpose of tearing down the present police headquarters and building something fit for people to work in. If the existing conditions were found in a penitentiary, or a slaughterhouse, plenty of good citizens would be stirring up the authorities to examine their consciences and dig into the vaults. But as the sufferers were only the people who made it reasonably safe for them to sleep in their beds at night, nothing was done. Half a century of sweat and grime seemed to have soaked into the peeling walls.

The Homicide Bureau was allotted three rooms on the third floor. Two of the doors presented battered wooden faces to the world, but the third had the distinction of being half-panelled in dirty frosted glass. This was the one I wanted, the one which usually housed Rourke and Randall.

I tapped and went in, closing the door behind me. Rourke was bent over some papers, his iron grey hair bristling. When he realised I hadn't gone out again, he looked slowly up.

'What do you want, Preston?'

'Just some information if you've got a minute.'

'A minute?' he smiled dangerously. 'Why, Preston, I have all the time in the world, naturally. And I'm anxious to place it at your disposal.'

The door behind me opened and closed. Detective Schultz went and sat at Randall's desk.

'Schultz,' beamed Rourke, 'Preston here wants to know if I've got a minute. Have I got a minute, Schultz?'

Schultz had evidently been getting more than his share of Rourke's rasping tongue. Nervously, he said,

'Whatever you say, lieutenant.'

Rourke tutted with disappointment.

'What do you suppose Schultz is doing here, Preston?'

'Pinch—hitting for Randall?' I hazarded.

'H'm, m'm,' he confirmed. 'Detective Schultz is standing in for Sergeant Randall. The sergeant is in hospital, did you know that? And why is the gallant defender of the peace in the hospital? Was he shot down by some crazed hoodlum? No. Is he suffering from years of nervous strain, overwork and lack of sleep? No. He has the mumps. A grown man, thirty-five years old, he has the mumps.'

'They say it can be very painful,' I pointed out.

'They do, huh?'

He turned and looked at Schultz.

'Well, what happened?'

'There were two of them, one eighteen, one seventeen. We picked them up while they were packing to leave town. The younger one still had the gun in his pocket.'

Rourke nodded.

'Good. Very good. Do they want to talk?'

'Whether they want to or not, they'll talk,' replied Schultz.

'Better. Even better. So what are you doing here?'

Schultz shifted uncomfortably.

'I can't start an interrogation on my own authority on a major offence. Have to get the O.K from a sergeant or higher.'

Rourke said very quietly,

'But I sent a request three days ago for you to be temporary sergeant.'

'I know you did, lieutenant. The paper's still stuck in the machine higher up.'

'O.K, O.K. You have my authority to get on with it.'

'Thanks.'

Schultz got up, pushed past me and went out.

'Well, since Schultz seems to have nailed that one down, maybe I can give you a minute. Siddown.'

I sat. The lieutenant leaned back and opened the box which lay by his right hand. It was half-filled with a singularly noxious variety of thin Spanish cigars. He rolled one round between his lips quickly, lit it, and ejected a thick poisonous cloud of yellow smoke into the already heavy atmosphere.

'What's it all about, Mark?'

'Hope I'm not wasting your time,' I said, and I meant it. 'There was a car smash two months back. Boy named Jeff Hawkins got killed. He was junked up at the time, and I thought you probably had a look at it to see whether everything was on the level.'

He nodded.

'Yup. Did it myself. What about it?'

'Was there any possibility it could have been anything else but what it seemed? I mean Hawkins had never stepped out of line in his life. It seems a lot of crazy things to go and cram into your last half-hour on earth.'

His head was only vaguely visible now through the swirl of pungent tobacco smoke. It was beginning to make my eyes smart.

'You'd never make a cop, not on my squad,' he advised. 'That crack about crazy things just before somebody decides to die. That's exactly the time they do decide to get a lot of weird stuff out of their systems. I remember this Hawkins thing. Open and shut. He was the only one in the car. There was no possibility of anyone having jumped out within a reasonable period before impact. He had almost as much heroin as corpuscles in his circulatory system. And he did steal the car. Tell me why you want to know.'

'His brother got back from a sea trip today. He's a sailor. He says the whole thing is crazy, and he's paying me to dig into it.'

The fierce eyebrows lifted, and the piercing eyes raked over my face.

'If anybody else said that to me I'd swear they were putting me on. His brother says that, does he? I know you're not too bright sometimes, Mark, but I would have thought even you would be used to the reactions of the sorrowing relatives. Naturally he thinks it crazy. But I'm telling you it happened, just the same.

In self-defence I lit an Old Favourite. The grey smoke was enveloped and strangled scornfully by the wreathing fumes from the lieutenant's weed.

'I'm not suggesting it didn't happen,' I returned evenly. 'And nor, to my surprise, is

58

the brother. What he wants me to find out is why. This was a quiet guy, this Jeff. Everybody says so, and everybody ought to know. The brother thinks there had to be something in his life he kept from everyone, something which was ultimately responsible for what happened. That's what I'm looking for.'

'M'm. Well, I wouldn't know about that. I was investigating a death following a car crash. All I had to do was satisfy myself everything happened the way it seemed. I wasn't interested in Hawkins, once I'd checked that nobody in the department had ever heard of him.'

That was one of the things I'd been going to ask.

'About the stolen car, can you give me anything on that?'

He got up and opened a file cabinet. After a quick rummage he came up with a thin file.

'Here it is. It was a this year's Packard, registered to an Albert F Augustin. He left it outside a place called the Beano Club. Next thing he knew, a highway patrol officer was telling him he'd need another car.'

'Nobody there saw Hawkins take the car?'

'No.'

'His brother was away at sea when it happened. Who'd you locate to identify him?'

He turned over the papers.

'Yes, I'm remembering this now. Best we could find at first was his boss at the place he worked, man named Ernie Kaplan. You know, that man wouldn't come to the morgue? He offered to help us in any other way we liked, but he said he couldn't stand the morgue. Put us in a spot for a while. Took us best part of a day to track down the girl-friend.'

'She identified him?' When he nodded, I asked, 'Who was she?'

'Name of Susan Hofmeyer. Nice kid, pretty. With all the riff-raff you meet in this job, it's a real pleasure to talk to somebody like that, once in a while. Could have been one of my own girls.'

From Rourke, that was as high a compliment as you could expect for anybody. Susan Hofmeyer had made an impression. Rourke looked at his watch pointedly.

'You said a minute, Mark. I can't sit here gabbing it up with you, while one half the city's out butchering the other half. Anything else you want?'

'No thanks, John, that about covers it.'

I got up to leave.

'Oh, one other thing. Did you ever hear of the Elman brothers?'

'Elman.' He stared at the ceiling. 'Elman. No. Why, should I?'

'Not necessarily. Thanks.'

As I walked down the passage I could hear the rapid questions being fired at the two suspects Schultz had picked up.

I drove slowly back to Parkside Towers. At least that was my intention. But my stomach was complaining about the famine conditions, so I stopped off at a late diner for a sandwich and a glass of milk. As I sat chewing, I reflected on all the progress I was making in checking into Jeff Hawkins death. With all the people I'd talked to, all the fog I'd swallowed, I knew exactly as much as when I started. Well, tomorrow there'd be more people, maybe even more fog. I left some money on the counter and went back into the street. As the closing glass door shut off the warm interior of the diner, somebody pushed me hard to one side. I stumbled into the fog and somebody else grabbed my arms.

'A drunk,' said a voice.

'Get him off the street,' said another.

I wasn't in a position to do much about it. Each arm was now held by a different man. Unless my ears were playing tricks there was a third walking behind us. They pulled me down the narrow alleyway that ran along the side of the diner.

'Too much with the questions, peeper. Too

much with the nose.'

Steel fingers reached over my head and jerked cruelly at my nose. At the same moment my mouth was forced violently open. I wanted to throw up, and couldn't. Something like ice in my mouth. Ice with a sharp edge. If I could have made a sound it would have been a scream of fear.

'You feel it, huh, peeper? Steel cutters. The best.'

The cold steel moved slightly. There was a small sharp pain at my tongue and something warm ran into my mouth.

'Suddenly you don't wag your tongue so much, eh?'

My chief tormentor chuckled, an evil wet sound. 'This is just a friendly tip. You keep your fat mouth shut, or we'll be back. And next time, we cut out your tongue.'

The coldness went away, at least from my mouth. The sick cold of fear remained in my stomach. Then the hands at my face relaxed. I knew what had to come next, but there was nothing left in me to stop it. There was blinding agony as a foot crashed into my groin. As I fell somebody punched expertly at the back of my ear. I hardly felt it. I was through long before the punch landed. The paving of the alleyway seemed almost soft as I hit it. Then all the lights went out.

Somebody was trying to pick me up. No, wait a minute. Somebody was trying to take my coat off. No, that wasn't it either— Somebody was putting a hand in my inner jacket pocket. Yes. Feebly I grabbed for the hand. As my fingers touched it, some of my strength returned, and I managed to hold on. Twisting, I stared into the face above me. A frightened, dirty face, with thick grey stubble over it. His breath nearly put me out again. For some reason I was on my back in an alleyway. This human derelict was picking my pockets. Irritably I climbed to my feet, still hanging on to the bag of bones. Holding him at arms length, I checked my pockets. My cigarettes were gone.

'Let's have the butts,' I snapped.

'Honest, mister—'

I showed him my fist. Quickly, he dived into a pocket and brought out the pack. He was dribbling with fright, and I felt disgusted. What was the matter with me, anyhow? Getting tough with this ruin, while the guys I should have been looking for were probably miles away, laughing their heads off. I released my grip.

'Keep 'em.'

'Gee thanks—' he began.

'Beat it.'

He scuttled off into the fog.

I made my unsteady way back to the car and headed home.

CHAPTER 6

It was after 9.30 next morning when I rolled into the office. I was in good shape, aside from the yellowing bruise behind my left ear, and the fact that somebody had left a trip-hammer inside my skull. Florence Digby stopped typing long enough to look first at me, then the clock in a pointed way.

'*Good* morning, Mr Preston,' she greeted coolly. 'Shall I get some bromide?'

'Miss Digby,' I returned stiffly. 'The reason I look the way I look is because of devotion to duty. Look at this.'

I presented my left ear, with decoration. She glanced at it and if it impressed her, she could have fooled me.

'There was a telephone call a while ago. A man,' she announced. 'He wouldn't leave any name. Said he'd call again later.'

'O.K,' I grunted. I was peeved because I didn't get any sympathy over the ear. 'I want Sam Thompson, if you can find him.'

Sam Thompson is a guy I sometimes use when he's available. I don't mean available for work, which is any time, but available for performing some endeavour which entails a cash payment. Sam does not like work, and the lengths to which he will go to avoid it would have made a more orthodox character a millionaire years before. But no work, no eat is one of the cornerstones of civilisation, so whenever the hunger pangs are becoming acute, Sam comes out of his hole and hires out. Florence Digby was one of the few people who usually knew where to find him.

I'd only just settled at my desk when Florence buzzed.

'Sam will be here within fifteen minutes,' she informed me.

'Good. One of his lean periods, huh?' I replied, but she'd already broken the connection.

I was in the middle of the sports section of the *Globe* when he arrived. He shuffled in suspiciously, looked quickly around to ensure there wasn't anything in sight that needed doing, then perched on a chair by the wall.

' 'Lo, Preston,' he sighed. 'If it's anything

65

hard, count me out.'

' 'Lo, Sam,' I replied. 'It isn't hard. Mostly it consists of a nice-looking doll.'

He cheered up slightly.

'Good legs?' he queried.

'The best. You can look at 'em all you want.'

'I don't do it for nothing just the same,' he growled suspiciously.

'You'll get your money,' I assured him. 'You know the Oyster's Cloister?'

'Ben Krantz's joint? Sure.'

'Across the street from there is a delicatessen. Name of Miller's. The girl works there. She's around twenty years old and her name is Susan Hofmeyer. I want to know about her. Everything you can get.'

'Where she goes, I go?' he queried.

'Right.'

'I'll need expenses extra.'

'You got 'em. Don't let her know what's going on.'

He looked pained.

'If I had any professional pride, or any other kind for that matter, that crack would have hurt. All the years I've been legging these streets, not once did anybody ever spot me.'

If it was an exaggeration, it was a small one. Thompson has a very high reputation as a legman. I looked apologetic.

'Phone me tonight with what you get,' I instructed. 'I may be out but keep calling till you get me. Can do?'

'Can do,' he confirmed. 'Er—'

'Here's ten.' I held the bill across the desk. He grinned nervously, then shuffled over to collect. 'There'll be more if and when you need it.'

He stared disappointedly.

'You're taking plenty of care I don't go to Catalina and whoop it up, ain't you?'

I made it five more and that had to satisfy him. The door had hardly closed when it was open again. Standing looking at me was Vince Brooks.

'I hear you're looking for me?' he queried.

'Not exactly, Vince, but it's always nice to have the Fraud Squad drop in. Makes the other tenants feel I have a nice solid business here.'

He grinned and sat down.

'Wasn't that Sam Thompson I passed outside?' he asked innocently.

'You know it was Sam Thompson. You know that I know you know it was Sam Thompson. If you think I'm going to tell you why he was here, you're out of luck.'

He shrugged. Brooks doesn't look like anybody's idea of a police officer. He is a slim dapper man, darkly handsome, and a smooth dresser. Lots of people take him for an actor, and maybe they're not far wrong at that. The detection of fraud is frequently an intricate and lengthy business. Often is was necessary for Brooks to involve himself with the con men, or whoever it was, passing himself off as a citizen with a weakness for the fast buck. Now he sat regarding me calmly, as though he'd dropped by for afternoon tea.

'Who said I wanted to talk to you?' I asked.

'You asked John Rourke about the Elman boys,' he replied. 'Anybody who shows any interest in those guys wants to talk to me.'

'O.K. What've you got?'

He made a hurt face.

'Preston, doll, this is not the way it goes. I'm the policeman, remember? You talk first, then I may, I say may, talk to you.'

He smiled his nice white teeth at me. I hunched my shoulders.

'What I have is nothing, probably.'

I told him about my interest in Jeff Hawkins. The way I told the story the Elmans just happened to be at the Cloister, and as they were strangers I asked about them. I didn't mention that my client Frank Hawkins, was with them at the time. Brooks listened attentively, said nothing till I was through.

'That's the only reason you were interested in those guys, because you didn't know them,' he asked suspiciously.

'I know most of the crowd over there,' I said defensively. 'Anybody from outside who might have had any connection with the Hawkins boy naturally interests me. I told you I didn't have anything. That's why I'm clutching at straws this way.'

He didn't quite believe me and I couldn't quite blame him, but he made no more protests.

'Clutching you may be,' he wagged his head, 'but straws those guys are not. Straws you can get hold of. Trying to hold those two is like grabbing two handfuls of oil.'

'Slippery, huh? Like to enlarge on it?'

He hesitated. Then,

'Well, I suppose it'll do no harm to talk some. I don't altogether buy your story, but I'll say this. If those guys are involved in something, anything, I think you'll tip me off. I know you and the department don't always see eye to eye, but in your own twisted fashion I think you try to be on the same side we are. So I want the Elmans, and you can maybe put them my way. And so I'll tell you about them.'

I got big-hearted with my Old Favourites and

Brooks came and sat nearer the desk.

'These two beauties came out this way from the east. That was a little over three years ago. They weren't criminals, not convicted criminals at least. They were the kind we refer to as 'known to the police'. When we say that it usually means we nearly had our hands on them twenty times, but they always had that extra something in the tank. Back there they did all kinds of things, but they were never in the hardware business. They hadn't been in Monkton more than a month before they owned a hardware store. The previous owner had had the business more than twenty years. It wasn't what you'd call a big concern, but it had standing. Suddenly the guy moved out and the Elmans moved in. And you know something?'

I didn't know something. Brooks spoke slowly and emphatically.

'There isn't any record that the Elmans paid any money for the business at all. The previous owner, we'll call him Smith, had always had his legal affairs taken care of by one of our local firms. But they didn't come into the transaction when the business was transferred to the Elmans. The whole thing was done by an eastern firm. The local man came to see me. He thought there was a bad smell somewhere, and I agreed with him. I talked to Smith, but he told me it was none of my affair, which was true. He said he had made a perfectly legitimate deal with the Elmans and nobody outside had any right to question it. That was true too.'

'Sounds as though the Elmans may have had something on this Smith,' I suggested. 'Something big enough to make him give up the store without a murmur.'

'That's what I thought,' nodded Brooks. 'In fact I was convinced of it. Still am. But I've never been able to turn anything up.'

'And this is why you'd like to put the arm on these two boys?'

He grinned.

'Be your age, Preston. If I went out gunning for people every time I didn't understand a business transaction, I'd have to be some kind of nut, no?'

'Yes,' I agreed. 'I thought it didn't sound like you.'

'Thank you. Compliments already.' He spoke lightly, but he was pleased. 'No, the way they started was enough to make me take an interest in them, and that was all. But for two guys who knew nothing about hardware, they were certainly quick learners. All of a sudden people needed their merchandise. People who'd never dealt with the store before started pouring in business. This took a big bite out of the other dealers' bread, so they had the Fair Trading Commission look into the Elmans.'

'And nothing,' I hazarded.

'Right. A man has the right to buy where he wants. If he wants the Elman's stuff, that's his affair. The Commission gave them a clean sheet. That made them ambitious. Last year they had a fire. Twenty thousand dollars worth of stock destroyed, they claimed. You can imagine, I'd been waiting for something like it. Once I got the insurance beef I moved in there with the best men I could muster. And I can see by your face you already worked out how far it got me.'

It was my turn to nod.

'They seem to be a couple of smart characters.'

'Pah,' he snorted. 'Smart. Well, maybe in a sense. Smooth, certainly. Cy, he's the one with whatever brains they possess. The other one, George, he wouldn't be able to run a news stand by himself. The guy is practically a moron. Anyhow that's the Elmans. That was what I wanted you to know. And I want them. Any contribution you care to make will be received with gratitude.'

'Tell me,' I asked. 'When I talked with Joe

Carpenter he said these birds didn't have very good credit. If the business is so successful, never mind how that's achieved, it seems to me they could raise credit easily enough.'

Brooks flicked ash into a tray.

'Joe was exaggerating. What he should have said was, the legitimate trading houses don't like the Elmans. Nobody would exactly trip over rushing to help them. But not everyone is so ethical as Joe likes to think. They could raise credit all right if it was necessary.

'Well, that's all I have, Preston. Now you've heard it, does it help you remember anything else you meant to tell me?'

'No,' I denied. 'I'm afraid not. I'll probably never see or hear of either of them again. But if I ever do hear anything that you'd like to know, I'll certainly tell you.'

He sighed, and got up.

'I'm disappointed. I was hoping you were going to dump some nice incontestable evidence in my lap. Something that would mean a nice seven to fourteen for each of them.'

I made noises about being sorry I couldn't be more help, and after a few minutes more chatter, Brooks left.

I sat for a while mulling over what he'd told me, and wondering what connection there was between the brothers and my client. It had been no particular surprise that Hawkins had pretended not to know me at the Cloister. That was a part of his intricate theory that I ought to appear to be interested at the instigation of somebody other than himself. I flicked down the intercom switch.

'Miss Digby, I want to locate a man named Albert F Augustin. Will you find out where he lives, and anything else about him?'

'Right away,' she replied.

One of the expenses you incur in this business is the purchase of an astonishing variety of reference books. Most of them get out of date quickly enough to need reissuing each year, and the annual expense is considerable. But when you want to know who and what somebody is, that's when one or more of the books pays for itself. It took Florence Digby about twenty minutes to produce a stack of information about Mr Augustin that might have surprised him.

He was on the board of five companies, two chemical, two textile and one boot and shoe manufacturer. He was sixty-three years old and had volunteered for service with the Navy in the Second World War. He collected some shell fragments at Iwo Jima and was invalided out a few months later. He was an enthusiastic golfer, and a member of two of the most exclusive clubs in Monkton City. He'd been married twice. The first wife had died several years before. The second was his total compensation for a large sum of money he lost backing a musical show that never finished its first week's run. The lady had a big part in the show, but had retired from the business when she married him. He had two children from the first marriage, a man of thirty-one and a girl aged twenty-eight. There was nothing in any of the books to indicate their opinion of their step-mother, who was several years younger than either of them. Augustin had an office downtown and I asked Florence to get them on the telephone. There was a girl at the other end, pleasant but impersonal.

I asked for Augustin.

'I'm sorry, but he's left for the day,' she told me. 'Who is that speaking, please?'

'My name is Preston,' I told her. 'It's a personal thing. Can I reach him at home?'

'Well,' she demurred. 'Mr Augustin doesn't like to have his home used for business, these days.'

'But he has gone there?' I pressed.

'Yes,' She was reluctant to admit it. 'You did say this was a personal matter?'

'I did. I'll try his home. Thanks.'

I sat and looked out at the bright sunshine

with distaste. The way it was carrying on out there, nobody could have guessed it had been absent from duty the whole of the previous day, leaving the city at the mercy of that filthy fog. If the fog had still been around I'd have telephoned Augustin's home. But with the sun back, it seemed I had a pretty fair excuse for taking a ride out there. I told Miss Digby I'd be back after lunch, and left the office.

CHAPTER 7

Fifteen miles out from Monkton City, and heading inland is Lake Minaho. The original Indian name was something much longer that nobody could ever pronounce, but the English translation of it was The Water with the Beautiful Smile. Early settlers, after trekking west across the barren deserts for months without end, were said to have wept when they came to the lake. It wasn't a big one, just a few square miles, but the water was clear and pure, and filled with fine fish. The green edges of the lake had a good population of deer and other wild life, and it seemed to those pioneers that they'd found Paradise. Two or three small settlements quickly sprang up, and the place became famous as the last stopping point before the breakthrough to the Pacific. Nobody was certain where the name Minaho originated, but they were all so thankful not to have to attempt the tongue-twisting name the Indians had given it that they adopted the new title quickly. Later, when the Indian troubles were at their peak, the lake was too far from the larger communities for safety, and was left in peace again. Then, when things settled down, wealthy people who wanted to be out of town but not too far from their business interests, rediscovered Lake Minaho. They divided the area up into large sections and built fine houses out there. Today it is one of the most highly sought after residential areas in the southern half of the state.

The Augustin house was on the far side of the lake, with a private road cut through the forest to reach it. The road emerged suddenly from the trees and into almost a private world of well-kept lawns and shrubbery. The house itself was a disappointment, a large place which seemed to have been designed orginally for the express purpose of reminding the visitor at every turn that this was the residence of wealth and privilege. It was a sprawling, vulgar piece of pretension, and very typical of the building of the first ten years of the century. I had no difficulty in locating the front entrance. The entrance stood at the head of a flight of wide stone steps, plentifully sprinkled with stone columns to support an imposing canopy roof. All the imposing roof supported was an odd collection of statuary, eagles, lions, nymphs, a small boy blowing a horn and other ill-assorted roof-fellows.

There was a Cadillac and a Jaguar parked there, so I braked beside them and got out. I marched solemnly up the steps, undecided as to whether I was entering a museum or an ancient sun-palace of some pagan society. The great doors stood open, and there were no signs of life. I banged the brass tiger's head firmly two or three times, but the pagans took no notice. I stepped inside and called out. My voice came sadly back to me, but no other sound. I didn't want to waste my trip. The girl in Augustin's office had told me he'd left for home. He ought to be somewhere around. At the same time I didn't want a housebreaking rap thrown at me. I went back outside and tried again.

I walked out from the oppressive gloom of the canopy and made my way around the side of the house. At the side I was passing, one of the little architectural tricks was to frame all the windows with Norman arches, unless I'm getting my periods mixed. The result was that every room at ground level looked from outside like the library where the butler discovered the body. The sun was on the other side of the building and here I was in a wide strip of shade. The corner I approached had been rounded like one of those French castles. Just in time I stopped myself searching for the arrow-slits. I could see the smooth expanse of the rear lawns now, and as I came past the round tower I saw something which surprised me, though by now I should have expected it. Not fifty yards from the shore of one of the clearest and cleanest lakes in the world, somebody had built a huge swimming pool. The sun sparkled on the smooth blue surface and the white stone surround was almost too bright to look at. Not that I wanted to look at it. My attention was riveted on the golden body of the blonde. She lay on the immaculate grass close by the pool, her only protection against the beating sun consisting of two thin black strips of material, one up here and one down there. I could have enjoyed looking at her a lot longer, but the man kept blocking my view. He was another sun worshipper, and it grieved me to admit he had the body for it. Broad cleanly muscled shoulders tapering to a slim waist, and a rich dark brown colour all over. He and the blonde weren't what you call being distant with each other. In fact, the distance between them at any point would have been invisible to the naked eye. They wrestled silently on the lush grass, oblivious to the world. They didn't need the world right then, only each other. Especially they didn't need me.

I hated to break up the party, but I'd come to see somebody, and the grass would still be there after I left. Retracing my steps a few yards, I set up a loud whistle. I could never hold a tune when I whistled, but nobody ever suggested it wasn't loud. I stood still for five whole seconds then walked into view, still whistling.

The blonde was stretched out on one of those lounging chairs, all webbed plastic and aluminium. She seemed to be asleep. Muscle-boy was squatting beneath a rainbow-coloured beach umbrella, an open book on his knees. He looked in surprise towards the whistler. I walked up close, then said,

'Good morning. Hope you don't mind me coming round this way? I couldn't raise an answer at the door.'

He looked at me coolly. He had dark lean features and regular teeth. The black hair was crew cut.

'Did you wish to see somebody?'

I was certain the blonde was studying me covertly behind the huge sunglasses.

'Yes. Mr Augustin. Is he here?'

'Mr Augustin senior or junior?' he demanded.

'Senior,' I replied.

'No. As far as I know, he's at his office in town. Who are you?'

I ignored that.

'I phoned his office. They told me he'd left for home. He should have reached here before me.'

Involuntarily, his eyes flicked towards the blonde goddess.

'Are you asleep, Avis?'

She grunted, and made a good imitation of struggling into wakefulness.

'H'm, what is it, Charles?'

She leaned on one elbow, pretending not to be aware of how little coverage she was getting from the black nylon bra. I pretended not to be aware of it either. She looked at me with interest.

'Well, hallo,' she drawled idly. 'Do you come gift-wrapped?'

The body, the swimsuit and the surroundings were all upper tax-bracket, inherited wealth, class of pre-1929. The voice was Harbour

Street. Like so many more, Blondie did better when she kept her mouth closed.

'Avis,' said muscle-boy tightly, 'This man wants to see my father.'

So this was Charles Augustin, age thirty-one, recently presented with a new stepmother. Avis said.

'I'm sorry, Mr er—?'

'Preston, Mark Preston,' I supplied.

'—sorry, Mr Preston, my husband isn't here. He doesn't usually come home till late afternoon.'

And now I had the picture. Blondie was the stepmother. The beach boy was the son and Daddy didn't usually get home till late afternoon. At his age, a guy like Augustin Senior ought to have known better than to dump a package like that out in the sun to be collected in the late afternoon.

'I don't understand, Mrs Augustin. They told me at his office he'd already left to come home. I didn't drive fast, so he should have been here some time ago.'

'Perhaps I can help, Preston' Charles Augustin stood up, giving the tanned muscles plenty of action. 'What was it you wanted to see him about?'

I was glad to see he was an inch or so shorter than me.

'Your father's car was stolen a few weeks ago. The man who stole it killed himself.'

He nodded.

'I remember it well. The Packard. What about it?'

'I wanted to talk to him about that night, find out if there was anything unusual.'

'Unusual?' his voice became slightly edged. I wondered why. 'In what way, unusual?'

I shrugged.

'I've no idea. I'm just scraping up anything I can get. Vague theories, impressions. Anything.'

He looked at me pensively.

'Is one permitted to ask why it should be any of your concern?'

Avis stretched languorously and stood up beside me. I liked it, and Augustin didn't miss my reaction.

'Why, Charles, I've worked out the whole thing. Mr Preston here is from the insurance company. Albert hired that boy to steal the car and smash it up so he could collect the cover. Right, Mr Preston?'

She looked at me appealingly. I grinned.

'Not exactly. I don't know much about your husband, Mrs Augustin, but I'd venture a guess he doesn't need to play any tricks of that kind.'

'Absolutely,' snapped Charles, who seemed to feel he wasn't being allowed to take charge enough. 'Come on, Preston, what is all this nonsense?'

'I'm a private investigator,' I told him. 'I'm trying to find out what happened in the last few hours of Jeff Hawkins' life.'

'Hawkins, that was the man who stole the car, wasn't it?' he queried.

Avis answered for me.

'Of course it was. Funny thing was, Mr Preston, I knew him.'

'Knew him?' I repeated.

'You mustn't mind Avis,' interrupted Charles. 'Always dramatising. You didn't really know him at all, did you?'

'I did so,' she replied pettishly. 'He was a waiter at a place I used to go sometimes. Not a bad-looking boy, at that.'

'Avis,' said Charles sharply.

'Oh, you,' she pouted.

I didn't want to get mixed up in any quarrels. Quickly I said,

'That would be a place called the Oyster's Cloister?'

She smiled again.

'Why, yes, do you know it?'

'I've been there,' I nodded. 'Did you ever have any occasion to talk to him?'

'Really, Preston, this has gone far enough. Why should Mrs Augustin be interested in talking to waiters and people like that? I think you'd better go. My father isn't here.'

There was no mistaking the finality in Augustin's voice.

'Of course,' I said at once. 'Sorry to have been a nuisance.'

I turned to leave. Avis seemed to think it was a pity, judging by the expression on her face. Charles waited impatiently for me to move. It wasn't hard to guess the reason for his impatience.

'In case I pass Mr Augustin on the way back,' I said, 'Would you mind telling me what car he's driving? I would like to see him as soon as possible.'

'Cadillac,' replied Charles curtly.

I didn't move.

'Pale blue?' I queried.

'Yes. How did you know?'

'It was parked outside when I arrived,' I told him.

Avis gasped, and some of the blood drained from Charles' tanned face. Without a word, he turned on his heels and went into the house. The blonde watched his retreating back anxiously.

'If there's a chance of seeing Mr Augustin

Senior, do you mind if I wait a moment?' I asked.

She didn't seem to hear, I repeated the question.

Irritably she said,

'Wait, go, do as you damned please.'

At times of stress, evidently, Harbour Street quickly surfaced. She stood there, ignoring me entirely, squeezing her hands nervously together. She was thinking her husband may have seen the fun and games on the lawn from a window, and was probably wondering how she was going to talk her way out of it. I was wondering the same thing.

In less than a minute, Charles was back. If he'd seemed worried before, he was far more agitated now.

'Preston, will you come in a minute? No, not you, Avis. You wait out here.'

I walked towards the door. Avis flung herself past me and went to go inside. Charles held out his hands to restrain her.

'Something's happened,' she said breathlessly. 'Let me in there.'

'No,' he said. 'You can't help. Stay here.'

She struggled to get past. She was either going in, or one of us would have to keep her out by standing sentry.

'You stay with her,' I said. 'Which room?'

86

'Through the rear hall and the big door on your left.'

I went through the hall and located the door, which stood half-open. Albert F Augustin was an imposing figure. Even sitting down you could tell he must be six feet three or four inches tall. Thick silvery hair was swept imperiously back from the hawk-like features. His beautifully cut suit was immaculate, as was the light green shirt and the correctly knotted tie. In his breast pocket a monogrammed silk handkerchief was arranged with just the right touch of carelessness. The whole effect was that of a handsome elderly man with plenty of time and money to devote to his personal appearance. An appearance that was marred now by the ugly red stain which was spreading slowly over the breast pocket. I could forget any interviews with Albert F Augustin. He sat quite upright in the stiff-backed chair, the strong features relaxed now in death. I checked quickly around for the gun. There wasn't one in sight and that made it a matter for the homicide boys. Failing to locate a telephone in the room, I went back into the hall. Here I found one and called Monkton Headquarters. Rourke wasn't around but I got through to Schultz. He told me to stay where I was and keep everybody out of the room. Before going back outside, I lit an Old Favourite and stood thinking for a moment or two. I'm no ballistics man, but the gun that killed Augustin had been of fairly heavy calibre. I was sure of that. A weapon like that makes a noise when it goes off. I didn't know Charles Augustin or the dead man's wife, and either or both of them could have killed the old man for all I knew. But that didn't jell with the fancy wrestling they'd been putting in on the grass before they knew I was there. Plenty of people will kill, given the necessary motive and opportunity. But it's an unusual personality who can immediately get back to the romantic side of life. Augustin Senior had only been dead a short while, so it had to be one of those two. Or me. I suddenly realised how I was going to look to Schultz. I was Johnny-on-the-spot. I was the unexpected caller, the one who wanted to see Mr Augustin privately. Schultz wouldn't think seriously that I killed the old man, but the circumstantial evidence was such that I was a good jumping-off place for the investigation. Thinking cheerful thoughts I went back outside. The girl was sitting down on a picnic-chair, looking faintly worried. Charles was pacing up and down, smoking furiously. He swung round as he heard me.

'He's dead, isn't he?'

Avis caught her breath sharply. I nodded.

'Police are on their way,' I announced. 'We're to stop here and wait for them. Nobody goes into the room.'

He nodded vigorously, as though it was necessary to agree with anything I said. I perched on a chair and looked at the new widow.

'Mrs Augustin,' I said gently, 'I know this has been a terrible shock to you, but I'd like to suggest you go to your room and change. The police will want to talk to you, and after them the newspapers. I don't have to tell you the kind of coverage one or two of those will give this sad affair. And they will have cameras with them.'

'Good point,' said Charles crisply. 'Do as the man says, Avis. Put on something demure. If you have it.'

She flashed him a look that wasn't all sweetness and light, at the last sentence. Then she went slowly into the house.

'We have about twenty minutes at most,' I told Charles. 'We'd better use them.'

'Use them?' he looked at me uncomprehendingly. 'Use them for what?'

'To find out what gives,' I replied. 'That shot would have made a hell of a noise. How come you two didn't hear it?'

'I don't know,' he shook his head. 'We

89

were—talking. Maybe the sound of our voices—'

'No,' I interrupted decisively. 'You were not talking. I'd been here two or three minutes before you saw me.'

'Oh.'

He flushed deeply, the sudden blood darkening his neck below the ears. He flung away the half-smoked cigarette.

'Look, Preston, do you have to tell the police that? I know it looks pretty low after what's happened, but if my father hadn't— died, would it have seemed quite the same? My so-called step-mother is years younger than me. Why he wanted to marry a little tramp like that—'

'Whoa.' I held up a hand. 'You don't have to justify this to me. I'm just a guy who called to see your father. It isn't me you have to worry about, it's a tough stubborn Irishman by the name of Rourke. He'll be in charge of this investigation, and from here on the only thing important to you is what Rourke thinks. And if you're building up a mental picture of some dumb Irish flatfoot, get rid of it. This is a highly intelligent man, and he's been asking questions of interested parties for thirty years. Before he's through, he'll know more about you than you do, so if you take my advice you'll be on the level with him from the start.

He looked shaken.

'You mean, all this will have to come out? But what about my family, my business? I'll be ruined.'

It's a funny thing the way people imagine they can tramp around the world in their own sweet way, doing exactly what they think they'll do. Then, the minute it looks as if they're going to be found out, they start to holler about their poor sick mother, or what the boys at the club will say. And usually they expect it as no more than a right that everybody else is going to gather round and blow up a smoke screen. Charles Augustin was no different from a score of people who'd said similar things to me in the past. Always, be it noted, after they'd had their fun. I sighed.

'Look, Augustin, stop blubbering all over me. It's no fault of mine you're in this spot. For the record, I wouldn't lie to Rourke for you even if it would help. And believe me, it wouldn't. All it would do would be to make you look worse than you probably are, and it might cost my licence into the bargain.'

His lip curled.

'Hark to the moralist,' he sneered. 'How would your morals stand up to an offer of a thousand dollars to keep your mouth shut?'

Temper rose quickly in me, but I curbed it.

91

'I think you may not have said that if you hadn't just found what you did in there. If you like to say it again tomorrow. I'll push a few of your pretty teeth down your throat.'

He took a step towards me, checked, then turned his head away.

'Yes,' he muttered. 'That was raw. I'm sorry.'

'Forget it,' I replied. 'Look, none of this is my concern, but what I said just now was good advice. If you come clean with Rourke at the start, the chances are nobody else will get hold of the murky details. But if you make him dig for it, he'll have to go around asking lots of questions and so will other officers. The pieces will come out one by one, and that way you won't have a chance in hell of keeping it away from the press. Rourke you can trust implicitly, but you can't reasonably expect to trust half the city police force. Don't forget, your father was an important figure, certain newspapers would love it if they could spread a little dirt over this.'

He nodded, then suddenly put his face in his hands. I walked away, and stood staring down at the cool depths of the pool. My reflection stared up at me, an elongated figure with a thoughtful expression, as though wondering what it must feel like to be standing upright in the sun. Another reflection appeared beside mine. Augustin said,

'Sorry about that. I've just realised I ought to be calling people. This is important news in many ways. Especially Martha, my sister. She ought to be told at once. You think it will be all right?'

'Sure,' I confirmed. 'You'd better call her right away. Whether you tell anybody else is up to you. If you take my advice you'll leave it a while. Get the thing more in perspective before you do too much talking.'

He went away to the telephone. I realised suddenly he still hadn't accounted for not hearing the shot, but in the same moment I knew the answer. An answer, at least. The door to that study, or whatever they called it, was three inches thick. When I first arrived I'd put in some fairly active knocking on the front door. The noise of that hadn't penetrated to the back of the house. So it was a possible explanation that the gunshot had been effectively muffled by that heavy door. A sound behind caused me to turn. Avis Augustin was walking towards me, discreetly wrapped in an all-covering dark-blue dress.

'He's calling Martha,' she intoned irrelevantly. 'She hates me.'

I didn't want to get mixed in any more

Augustin family business.

'What will you do now, Mrs Augustin?' I asked.

'Do?'

'Yes. I mean, will you go on living here, or take a trip, or what?'

'Huh.'

The snort was far from ladylike.

'Well, at least you talk plain,' she said. 'I suppose you don't think I'm going to get any Oscars for my weeping widow act?'

I hadn't any comment on that either.

'What'll I do? What will I do?' she mused. 'Why I may go to Miami for the winter. Then I'll probably go to Europe, in my private yacht, naturally.'

The bitterness in her voice came as a surprise.

'Even if you can't run to a private yacht, I imagine you won't have to travel steerage,' I suggested.

'You do, huh? Is that what you imagine, Mr Preston? Well, let me tell you something. Outside of what I can steal from the house and a few pieces of jewellery, I shall be back where I started before I moved into this mink-lined prison.'

My interest quickened.

'You mean Mr Augustin's finances were in

bad shape?' I asked.

'Him? In bad shape for dough? That I'd like to see. The old skinflint had more gold than Fort Knox. We weren't talking about him, we were talking about me. And he didn't leave me a red cent. Nossir, not a red cent.'

I thought it was a little early in the proceedings to be talking about wills.

'You've seen the will?' I queried.

'Seen it, yes. I've seen it. He gave me a photostat copy of it so I wouldn't forget what it said. I'll quote you.'

She put her hands on her hips, screwed up her eyes while she concentrated.

'To my dear wife, Avis, who has in the last years of my life rekindled feelings I had almost forgotten, frustration, anguish, bitterness. I bequeath the sum of one hundred dollars.'

There didn't seem much I could offer by way of comment on that. Evidently the lawn-wrestling with Charles had not been an isolated instance, but merely the final episode in a series. I wondered vaguely who some of the other characters had been, and whether all of this had anything to do with the death of Jeff Hawkins.

Not that I had a lot of time for speculation, because the police arrived almost immediately. Schultz marched briskly out of the house, with

Charles Augustin tagging along behind.

'Lo, Schultzie,' I greeted. 'This is Mrs Augustin, the widow.'

'Sergeant Schultz,' he corrected. 'Good morning, ma'am. We'll try not to bother you any more than is absolutely necessary. Preston, the lieutenant wants you inside.'

I found Rourke in the room with the dead man, sitting opposite him and frowning.

'Tell me what happened,' he grunted.

I told him everything, including the grass bit. He didn't look at me while I was talking. This is an old trick of Rourke's, and it can be unnerving standing and talking away with no evidence that anyone is paying the slightest attention. People like to have an idea of how their story is being received, especially people who are giving forth a mixture of fact and fiction. From Rourke you get no reaction until the end, which is when he pokes his rasping voice in all the holes, and tears ruthlessly at a carefully constructed web.

'How long do you think he'd been dead?' he asked.

'I'm not qualified medically,' I reminded him.

'Preston,' he threatened. 'I think you're clean, I really do. But this is a corpse, and the city wants to know how he got that way. They pay me to find out and that's what I'm doing. You try to help me and you'll be out of here in twenty minutes. Get in my way and you'll spend the rest of the day downtown and maybe half the night as well. We can do this any way you say. How long had he been dead?'

'I'd say less than half an hour,' I said grudgingly. 'The blood was still spreading from the wound. And don't tell me you know a case where the blood was still spreading four hours after death. You probably do, but you asked for an unqualified opinion and I gave it to you.'

'H'm.'

He looked at the floor again. Seconds dragged by, while I tried to keep my eyes away from the dead man on the chair.

'The way you tell it,' Rourke said suddenly, 'You'd been here about fifteen minutes before they found him. So he was either killed while you were out there with the love birds, or else it happened just a few minutes before you got here.'

'That's right.'

'If it happened while you were here, those two beauties are in the clear, right? Did either of them come into the house while you were talking?'

'No.'

'Then they're in the clear for that period. So what have we got left? One of them, or both of them, came in here and killed the old man. Then, minutes later, the killer is outside playing the Adam and Eve scene. It's been done before sure, I have a case like it about ten years back, but it needs a special kind of person to do it, a kind any first year psychiatry student could pick out a mile away. And the son, Charles, he's not the kind. Not in my book. What about the girl? And don't tell me you're not qualified this time, or I'll call you a liar.'

I grinned slightly.

'About what you'd expect,' I replied. 'They gave her a double shot of hormones, held out on the brains.'

'Exactly. An empty-headed slut,' he concluded. 'You think she could have shot her husband, and then gone out there for the hay-rolling?'

'I'd say it was out of the question. She needed him alive.'

I told Rourke what Avis had said about the will.

'This house is isolated up this private road. The only way to get here is by car, unless you're one of these marathon walkers. You didn't pass any cars coming out. The only cars parked were the two you described. One of them belonged to the dead man, the other to the son. What's the answer?'

'One or other of the two men brought someone with him in the car. The someone killed the father—'

'—and is now hiding in the secret panel, waiting for everybody to go away, so he or she can walk the fifteen miles back into town,' he finished.

I shrugged.

'Well, what else have you got? Have you searched the house?'

'It's being done,' he snapped. 'Not that it means anything. I could hide a dozen people in a place this size, and they'd never be found by a search party of two, which is all I have. You think this ties in with that Hawkins thing you're working on?'

That was a typical Rourke manoeuvre. There was no change of emphasis in the conversational tone. He just slipped in the loaded question at the end. Fortunately for me, I wasn't trying to bluff him.

'I don't see why it should,' I replied. 'I've talked to a few people since I started, and all I know now is what I had at the beginning. Except, if anything, I'm even more puzzled about the way he died.'

Rourke was satisfied.

'Good. You should be. It puzzled me too, and there can only be one explanation. It took me two days to arrive at it, so you ought to make it in a week. Hawkins was a harmless, nice kid. Somebody talked him into trying a shot of the happy juice, and after that he didn't know what he was doing. That wasn't Hawkins behind the wheel, it was the big "H", and that has been the explanation of plenty more complicated situations than a straightforward car smash.'

He was probably right, and I had little doubt that would be the answer I'd come to in the end. But I still had a few questions to ask, a few people to see. And standing around looking at the dead body of Albert F Augustin wasn't getting me far.

'Could be,' I said. 'Is there anything else you want from me, John?'

'H'm? Oh, no. You can beat it if you want. Get into the office some time today and make out a statement about what happened here.'

'Sure. And, by the way, about the son.'

'What about him?'

'I advised him to tell you all about whatever's been going on between him and the wife. He's worried about it getting out. I told him if he came clean with you, and you were satisfied, you'd probably keep it to yourself.'

'That's what you told him, is it? Now I'll tell you something. I'm a police officer. I'm not a priest, or a doctor. Anything that has to come out in the course of an investigation will do so.'

'Sure, I told him that. Anything that *has* to come out,' I emphasised.

'O.K, O.K, I'll think about it. Send Mrs Augustin in.'

'In here?'

I looked significantly at Mr Augustin.

'Oh sure. Not in here. Tell her I'll be in the hall.'

I went out to the others. Charles looked at me anxiously.

'Lieutenant Rourke would like to talk to you, Mrs Augustin. He'll be in the hall.'

She nodded and went inside. Schultz was nowhere in sight, so that left Charles and me alone.

'What did he say, the lieutenant?' he asked. 'Who does he think did it?'

'Rourke doesn't tell anybody what he thinks,' I informed him. 'He asks questions and he files all the information, but what he thinks is anybody's guess.'

'I see.'

'He's told me I can go, and I'm going to do it before he changes his mind. Watch what you

101

say when the newshounds get here.'

'I will. And, Preston.'

'Yeah.'

'Thanks.'

He stuck out his hand. Suddenly I felt sorry for him. We shook briefly, and I left. In front of the house, two cars were drawing in, packed with all the boys from the department who would make cold scientific fact of the death of Albert F Augustin. A couple of them recognised me and waved.

As I eased off the brake and rolled away, I reflected bitterly on my strange trade. What kind of a life was it when I was recognised on sight by those whose business it was to paw over corpses? Whatever kind it was, I was stuck with it now. I turned my nose towards Monkton City and the matter of earning Frank Hawkins two hundred dollars.

CHAPTER 8

The sun was evidently ashamed of its dereliction of duty the previous day, it was now hitting double strength. The steaming concrete highway threw great chunks of heat at me all the way towards town, and I was glad I had such a short distance to drive. Just on the outskirts of Monkton a huge neon hoarding pointed out that it was just one half mile to the Beano Club. I hadn't been there since it got its new title a few months back. Before that it was the Black Jack and before that something else again. Every once in a while somebody sold, somebody bought. Out went the old bars, seating, decor and the rest, and in went the new ditto. Business would be brisk as everyone turned up to see the new paint job. Then it would ease into what passes for normal in that trade and after that would come the day when somebody would want to buy. Somebody with a great idea for giving the place a shot in the arm. Out would go the hula girls, the bamboo furniture, the carved tree images. In would come the matador waiters, the ironwork gates, the tango band. Last time it had been a cowboy saloon, and that had gone pretty well until the night the bandits came. They'd been cowboys, too. Everybody thought it was pretty funny, and a great publicity stunt. The bandits all had red masks, and they lined up all the revellers and took their wallets, jewellery and so forth. They even blew out the office safe with dynamite, and that was a great touch of realism. It was only when one of the waiters pretended to grapple with a bandit, and another member of the gang pretended to put three bullets into the waiter that the fun began to pall. The waiter put up a great show of having three holes in his back, and suddenly the realism became reality. After that episode, business fell off to the starvation level, and it was time for the interior decorators again.

As I turned into the curving driveway I wondered what the latest proprietor had installed. There was nothing on the outside to give a hint. Inside it was cool, and I saw the place was quietly decorated in a modern style, but without any gimmick theme. I located the bar by walking through a doorway that had 'Bar' written over the top, an object lesson for plenty of other places I could name. The bartender wore an ordinary cream jacket and I asked for a bottle of cold beer. When he set it up I said,

'Haven't been here in months. Who's the manager now?'

'That's Mr Foyle,' he told me.

'Foyle,' I repeated. 'Would that be Edward Foyle?'

'No, sir. This is Mr Calvin Foyle.'

I thanked him and sipped at the beer. It was good. I wondered whether the crazy idea I was turning over was prompted by any real purpose, or whether I was letting the heat annoy me too much. There was a way to find out. I finished the beer with regret.

'Where do I find him, Mr Foyle?' I demanded.

The barkeeper pointed.

'Through that door and the second room on your left.'

'Thanks.'

I went in the direction indicated and found the door. It said 'Manager—Private'. I opened it and went inside. A man sat in a comfortable cane chair by a window. He had some papers on his knee and was making marks with a pencil.

'You have the wrong room,' he told me.

He was a tubby character, with sandy hair and a flabby face. The eyebrows were so close to the colour of his forehead that they were hardly visible at all in certain lights. Like now. The result was to give him a look of unhealthy and permanent surprise. He wasn't a character I could take to on sight.

'I don't think so,' I said, sounding as insolent as possible. 'You Cal Foyle?'

'I am Calvin Foyle,' he replied icily. 'Who are you and what do you want?'

'Don't be that way, Cal, I'm here to do you a favour.'

He looked at me with deepening suspicion, and kept looking at the door as if hoping for an interruption. Now he put his papers aside and looked at me.

'Why?'

'Why should I do you a favour?' I said. 'Because you may be in a position to do a little something for me.'

He grunted.

'At least that makes a little more sense. For just a second, I thought you were going to do something for nothing.'

I grinned.

'Nobody does anything for nothing.' I pointed out. 'Me least of all.'

'Before I have you thrown out,' he said pleasantly, 'Who are you?'

'Name of Preston, I'm a P.I.'

'A what?'

'A private investigator,' I explained.

'Oh, one of those. Sorry, no keyholes today.'

I sighed.

'Cal, let me be frank with you. You may be a whizz as a manager of this kind of place, but you weren't cut out for the rough stuff.'

His eyes flickered nervously.

'What do you mean by that? Are you threatening me?'

'Pshaw,' I scoffed, 'I'm here to do you a

favour. A couple of months ago, a car was stolen outside this place. Remember?'

'You talk in circles,' he snapped. 'Cars get stolen out there at the rate of one per week.'

Then, realising that wasn't very good advertising, he said quickly,

'That is, we've had more than one car stolen. Which one do you have in mind?'

'One a week?' I raised my voice questioningly. 'That's bad for business. But you'll remember this one, Cal. This one especially. Because this one belongs to a prominent man, Albert F Augustin.'

He nodded.

'Certainly, I remember the occasion. What about it?'

'This about it. Augustin died this morning. He didn't die a natural death. I just left his house crawling with policemen. They're going to be coming to see you again, Cal.'

He swallowed, but I couldn't tell whether from nervousness or because his throat was dry.

'Why would they want to do that?' he demanded. 'I told them the little I know at the time.'

'Maybe, maybe,' I conceded. 'But they might not think so. Especially if I had a talk with them.'

He squinted at me thoughtfully.

'I haven't the faintest idea what you're talking about. How did Augustin die, as a matter of interest?'

'It is a matter of interest,' I agreed. 'To a lot of people. He died of a gunshot wound. He wasn't pretty.'

Foyle stared out of the window. It was time to go. I dropped a card in his lap, and he stared down at it.

'I haven't talked to the police yet,' I told him. 'I wanted to come here and do you this favour first. If you want to do any little thing for me, call me at one of those numbers. Don't leave it too long, because it's my duty as a citizen to tell the law what I know. And I'm a great little one for duty.'

He didn't look up as I went out of the room. I'd only called on him on an impulse. That's how I do a lot of things. Most of them turn out to be a fat waste of time, but every now and then the three oranges drop in a straight line.

Nobody had stolen my car, and twenty minutes later I walked into the office. Florence Digby pretended not to notice me.

'Afternoon, Miss Digby,' I greeted.

She looked up in feigned surprise.

'Why, it's Mr Preston, isn't it?'

'Don't ride me, Florence, it's too hot,' I grumbled.

'Well, I'm sorry, Mr Preston. I certainly didn't intend to be riding you. It's just that it's a very difficult matter working in an investigation agency, when the investigator puts in so little time on the job. How you imagine I can keep track of what's going on round here—'

'Is something going on?'

Her lips pursed primly.

'You could say that. That man's been on the telephone again twice, the one who won't leave his name. Two newspapers have called, and a man from the *Clarion* even came to the office. He wouldn't believe you weren't here until I actually showed him your desk.'

'They're interested because I found a dead man this morning.'

I told her about what had happened at the Augustin house. At least I told her most of it. The part about Charles Augustin and his step-mother I left out. Florence is one of those good listeners. She doesn't make any comments, doesn't pull any faces while you're talking. The experience is restful and exhilarating, if that makes any sense. It's restful, because you unburden your mind of a clutter of scattered facts, half-truths and impressions, all of which have been dropped in at random, an untidy heap of information. Exhilarating, because even as you're talking you find you have subconsciously classified certain sections, and some of the information has filed itself. Not in the willy-nilly style it was received, but under certain broad headings. It's like that second evening on the king-size jigsaw puzzle, when you sit back and realise that already you have the vague outlines of one of the corners, a task which seemed beyond you when you first broke open the box. Not that a jigsaw is really a fair subject for comparison. With one of those you at least start out having all the pieces. With the little puzzles I get, you start with one or two pieces, and no indication of how many it takes to make the picture.

But as I talked to Florence Digby, I realised there were already two or possibly three outlines of ideas forming in my mind, a position I couldn't have envisaged twenty-four hours earlier.

'Well, what do you make of it?' I asked her.

'There isn't a great deal to make much of, is there?' she countered. 'Do you think Charles Augustin killed his father?'

That was one of the things I'd been trying not to think.

'I'm not concerning myself too much with

that,' I hedged. 'Rourke is working on it, and with so few people involved I imagine he'll produce the answer in no time at all. No point in my worrying about it from this distance.'

'H'm. I must say, I don't like the sound of this Mrs Van Dorn.'

'Oh, I don't know why I bothered to mention her,' I replied. 'She isn't really in this at all.'

The telephone rang. Florence answered it. Then she said,

'Just hold the line one moment, please,' and held out the receiver.

'She's in it now,' she said nastily.

I leaned down and held the phone to my ear. 'Mrs Van Dorn?'

'Is that Mark Preston? The one who was here last night?'

She sounded mean and bad-tempered.

'The same,' I confirmed. 'What can I do for you?'

'You can get over here about as fast as you can run,' she snapped. 'My apartment has been torn to pieces, and you'd better get something done about it.'

'Your apartment,' I mumbled. 'I'm sorry, Mrs Van Dorn, I'm tied up on another matter right now. I can recommend—'

'You get here,' she yelled. 'This is all your doing.'

The receiver was slammed down at the other end with a force that made my ears jangle.

'Bad connection,' asked Digby sweetly.

I glared at her.

'That woman's crazy.'

But I knew I was going. Her apartment had been wrecked, and something had made her say it was my doing. I didn't think I'd made such a big hit with Julie Van Dorn that she'd try a stunt like that just to get me over there. And anyhow, a girl with what she had on the ball didn't need any intricate device of the kind to bring the boys a-running. All she needed to do was snap her fingers.

'I'm going out,' I told Miss Digby.

'Naturally,' she observed.

'I'll be at—'

'Mrs Van Dorn is listed,' she informed me.

And that didn't do anything to improve my frame of mind. Soon I was back outside 1616 Alohah Apartments. The pretty maid looked worried as she showed me in.

'What are you going to do about all this?' was the greeting I got from her enraged mistress.

'All this' was as complete an attempt as I'd ever seen to turn an elegant apartment into a junk yard. Anything that could be emptied, had been emptied. Anything that could be toppled over was face down on the floor. The inside of the record player had been ripped out, and there were torn cushions everywhere. Astride the wreckage, or some of it, was as angry a female as I'd seen that day, in the person of Julie Van Dorn. Her attitude was one of such imminent aggression, I almost expected the maid to sound the bell for the start of the first round.

'Anything missing?' I demanded.

'How do I know,' she shouted. 'I haven't looked.'

To the maid, I said,

'Check around, would you? Just for the obvious things, like jewellery, furs, any cash Mrs Van Dorn keeps here.'

She nodded and went to work. Julie watched without comment, I didn't blame her for being mad, but I also knew we weren't going to make any progress if we stood around yelling at each other. I bent down and picked up a chair, set it on its legs again. Then I got another one and did the same.

'Sit down, Mrs Van Dorn,' I told her crisply.

'Sit down?' she roared. 'What do you mean, sit down?'

'I mean sit down,' I snapped. 'All you're

doing at the moment is to make a lot of noise, and it's getting us exactly nowhere. Do as I tell you and sit down.'

To my surprise, she gave one more snort then plumped heavily down. I sat too and pulled out my Old Favourites.

'Now, tell me exactly what happened.'

'You can see what happened,' she said irritably.

'All I can see is that the room is a shambles,' I corrected. 'It doesn't tell me anything. But you can. Where were you while all this was going on?'

'Out, naturally. Do you imagine I'd have stood by while they did this to my beautiful furniture?'

I ignored that.

'Out where and at what time?' I pressed.

'It's Heather's birthday—' she began with an attempt at patience.

'—Heather?' I queried.

'That's me.' The maid stuck her head round the door and smiled shyly.

'Happy Birthday, Heather. Please go on, Mrs Van Dorn.'

'I wanted her to have a present, a brooch. But you know, or maybe you don't know, what one woman thinks is pretty, another one will hate. So I suggested we go together to buy it.'

I nodded.

'You left the apartment together to buy Heather's present. At what time?'

'Two o'clock, two fifteen,' she guessed.

'No, Mrs Van Dorn,' corrected Heather. 'It was one forty-five as we went out.'

'Very well, it doesn't matter.'

'It does matter,' I corrected. 'It might matter a great deal. We don't know yet. You went out at one forty-five. What time did you return?'

She thought more carefully this time.

'At three twenty.'

We both waited for Heather to contradict her, but there was no bid.

'Tell me what happened when you came in.'

'Well, we came in the door, and saw how everything was. For a second or two we couldn't believe it, either of us. Then, well we went a little crazy, dashing all round the place to see if every room was the same.'

'And they all were?'

'They all were,' she nodded. 'For a minute or two I was too, what shall I say, stunned, shocked, to register that this had really happened to me.'

'Why didn't you call the police?'

'I did—at least, I should say, I was going to. As I went to pick up the telephone the damned thing started ringing. It was this man.'

'Man?'

'Yes. I didn't recognise the voice, but I'd know it again. It was horrible, soft and almost hissing, somehow evil.'

'What did he say, this man?'

'He said I was to ask you what this was all about. He also said if I called the police his friends would come here again. If they did my—my face would look the way the apartment looks.'

For the first time her voice faltered, and I realised she'd had a bad scare. But she wasn't looking for sympathy. At once, her voice was back to normal as she said,

'So start telling me what it's all about.'

I dragged deeply on the cigarette, and shook my head.

'I don't know. And that is the simple truth.'

She looked at me searchingly.

'I'd like to believe you, but how can I? After this, and what that man said?'

'Have you anything of great value here?'

'A couple of fur coats, and some small pieces of jewellery.' Raising her voice, she called. 'How did you make out, Heather?'

The maid came back into the room, shaking her head in puzzlement.

'I was just coming to tell you, Mrs Van

116

Dorn. I don't understand. As far as I can see, there isn't a single thing missing. Not a thing.'

Julie looked puzzled too.

'If nothing's been taken, why would they do all this?'

I disregarded that. I was trying to make up my mind about something.

'Heather, may I see your birthday present, please?'

Mystified, the girl went out into the hall. She came back rummaging inside a large crocodile hide purse. Taking out a small package, she held it out to me.

'Mind if I take off the wrapping?' I asked.

She shook her head, and gazed at Julie Van Dorn, who raised her eyebrows to indicate she too thought I was crazy. I pulled off the ribbon and paper and opened the small box. The brooch was in the shape of a scarab, neatly encrusted with small semi-precious stones.

'A very nice present. Thank you for showing it to me.'

I returned it to her. Julie tutted impatiently.

'I'm still waiting to hear what you've got to say about all this,' she reminded me tartly.

By way of reply I said,

'I don't know whether you're in the habit of drinking coffee at four in the afternoon, but

117

this would be a good day to start. Why don't you brew some up for all of us, Heather? I'm sure we could all do with it.'

'I don't—' began Julie.

'Please. We'll talk over coffee.'

'Oh, very well. Maybe it will settle our nerves, Heather. Do you mind, honey?'

'Certainly, Mrs Van Dorn.'

She went out, closing the door behind her.

'That was a pretty obvious trick,' Julie advised me. 'But you needn't have bothered. I'd trust Heather with my life, if I had to.'

'I'm sure you would, Mrs Van Dorn. And I'm sure you'd be justified. But I wouldn't trust her with mine. I don't know her and she doesn't know me. It looks as if we might be dealing with some people who play rough, and guys like that make no exceptions for women. If they got rough with Heather, she might die to protect you, but not me. She doesn't owe me a thing.'

'The point is, she's gone now, so start explaining.'

I took a deep breath.

'As I said before, I don't really know what's happening. The best I can produce is an educated guess.'

'And?'

'The people who did this think I'm holding

118

something they want. They either followed me here last night, or else they were told I was here. They must have thought there was a chance I'd left it with you, whatever it is. To-day they had this place watched until they knew both you and Heather were out, then broke in to search the place.'

She looked doubtful, and slightly mistrustful.

'What would be worth all that trouble?'

I heaved my shoulders.

'*Quien sabe?* Things have different values in different circumstances. It may not be worth a plugged nickel to anybody else. Maybe a let-ter, who knows?'

'A letter?'

'I'm only supposing. A letter could be the one thing the police need to complete a case against somebody on a serious offence, like even murder.'

'I think it's highly unlikely,' she sniffed suspiciously. 'And anyway whether it's a let-ter or what, why would anybody think you'd left it for me to hold? We're strangers.'

'Good point,' I agreed. 'And it tells me something. It tells me whoever did this is not anybody who knows either of us, or they'd know that.'

Her brow cleared slightly.

'Say, that's not bad thinking. Maybe you are

119

some kind of a detective, after all.'

'Not some kind,' I corrected. 'A private kind. That means I have no authority whatever, and everytime I get out of line I stand to lose my licence.'

'I don't follow that. Are you proposing to get out of line?'

'Let's say wide of centre,' I suggested. 'I'm going to ask you to do something the police department wouldn't approve of.'

'I'm listening.'

She was sitting in a more relaxed attitude now, no longer keyed up to such a pitch as when I first arrived.

'Your apartment has been broken into, and there's been damage. You ought to report to the police. I'm asking you not to.'

'Oh? Why?' she demanded.

'If I'm going to ask you this, I'll have to tell you something of the background. Did you ever hear of Jeff Hawkins?'

She thought for a moment.

'I don't think so. Should I?'

'Probably not.'

I told her how Jeff had died and a little of what had happened to me in the past twenty-four hours. She listened with great interest, interspersed with a minor barrage of questions.

'So far I haven't learned a lot,' I wound up.

'And most of that doesn't make any sense. But those guys who roughed me up last night made me think there has to be something to know. I wasn't even sure of that before. What somebody's done in here today, makes it seem there's also something to find. So we make progress.'

'Possibly. But what has this to do with my not telling the police?'

This was the delicate part.

'In the ordinary way, it isn't something I'd ask of a woman. Perhaps I should have said, it isn't something I'd ask an ordinary woman.'

She liked that bit, at least. Good.

'If you don't mind my saying so, Mrs Van Dorn, you don't scare easily. That's why I'm going to ask for your help. If you call in the police, these guys will stay out of your way. All that chatter on the telephone, that was just chatter. They won't come within a mile of you if they see a uniform.'

She shook her head.

'You don't make out much of a case for yourself, Mr Preston. Tough I may be, or may think I am, but if calling the police is going to prevent a repetition of this, I'm reaching for the telephone right now. You think I want to see those people?'

'No,' I confessed. 'I imagine not. But I do. By coming here, they've indicated that they think we're—er—acquainted. If you fail to scream for the law, they'll be sure of it. If they think they can get at me through you, they might show their hand. That way I'll get to know who I'm dealing with.'

She laughed.

'Cool. Very cool. You put me up on a fence, then you shout, 'Who wants to throw rocks at the pretty lady?' When the rocks arrive you peep over the fence to see who's doing the throwing. You'll no doubt correct me if I have the wrong impression.'

It would be a waste of time to try bluffing this girl.

'All right,' I nodded. 'I don't care for the way you put it, but it's close enough to the truth.'

She stopped laughing and looked at me seriously.

'But why should I do anything so crazy? And what makes you ask me?'

'Mrs Van Dorn,' I began carefully. 'I'm trying to find out why Jeff Hawkins died. I think I may be on to something.'

'You mean it was murder?'

I shook my head.

'No. I doubt that very much. At least, in the

ordinary definition I doubt it. But I think he was driven to his death, and that can amount to the same thing. He knew something or saw something he shouldn't. Maybe he even had whatever it was these guys were after today.'

'But if that were so,' she pointed out, 'Surely they would have got it back after his death?'

'I can't answer that one, or fifty questions that come to mind,' I admitted. 'But I still think I could be heading in the right direction.'

'I wouldn't know about that,' she replied. 'But you haven't answered my question. I never heard of Jeff Hawkins until today. Why should I voluntarily put myself in a position you admit to be dangerous.'

I swallowed.

'All right, I'll tell you. You may not like some of it, but that's O.K. Just don't get mad till I'm through. There's something phoney about the way Hawkins died, I'm sure of it. You could say that all I have adds up to something quite nebulous, and on the grounds of hard facts I'd have to agree. But today a prominent man, who was connected with the Hawkins death, also died. And under curious circumstances to put it mildly. Nothing nebulous about that. I have a strong hunch that these deaths are related. And before you shrug off one of my hunches, remember they are part of my business. If you care to check my credit rating, you will find business is good.'

She looked at me quizzically.

'All right up to now. But it doesn't sell me on my part.'

'I'm coming to it. Mrs Van Dorn, you have a lot of money. That's all right by itself, so long as you don't waste your life. And that's what you've been doing for some time past. You've been living, or half-living, in a state of idle luxury, and the accent goes on the "idle". You weren't trained that way by your father, I'll bet, and you don't really care for it too much. That's part of the reason you get your dander up so fast, because you're dissatisfied with your way of life. Now here is a chance for you to do something, something really useful. It could be uncomfortable, even dangerous, but you'll be living. Nobody will be kow-towing because you're *the* Mrs Van Dorn. Who you are won't make a scrap of difference to the people in this. All they'll be interested in is what you know. And even if we don't produce any results, it'll be a big break from what you've been doing.'

Except that she went slightly white at the corners of the mouth, she heard me out without a change of expression.

'Tell me one thing,' she whispered, 'What

124

gives you the right to come here and talk to me that way? Who do you think you are, some kind of higher authority sent down here to judge the lower animals?'

'No,' I replied simply. 'I'm a man who's trying to do a job. You can help get it done, and so I'm asking you. Will you?'

For a few seconds I thought I'd lost. Then,

'Very well,' she snapped. 'Don't think for a minute I accept any of that nasty little amateur analysis you gave me. I'm doing this for reasons of my own which are none of your affair.'

'But you'll do it?' I pressed.

'I'll do it. When do we start?'

'We already started,' I assured her. 'The fact that you called me over here immediately this happened, will have convinced the opposition they are doing the right thing. I've no doubt they're having this place watched.'

'You're a comforting person to have around the house,' she said tartly.

'Now what?'

I looked around me.

'The normal thing would be to ge something done about all this mess, wouldn't it?'

Heather came in with a tray of coffee. Julie said.

'I'll have to tell Heather what's going on. I

have no right to expose her to a situation like this without her knowledge.'

I bowed my head slightly. Julie told Heather she wouldn't be calling the police, and there was a chance the intruders might be back. If Heather wanted to bow out we would understand. Heather listened carefully, and thought for a moment before replying.

'I'd be lying if I said I was looking forward to it,' she said gravely. 'But I know I'd never forgive myself if anything happened to you, Mrs Van Dorn, and I'd gone off and left you alone. Still, I'd feel a lot better about it if Jack were here.'

'Jack?' I asked.

'Jack Wells, Heather's boy friend,' Julie told me. 'And a very good idea. Jack knows how to take care of himself. I'd like to have him here, too.'

'Fine,' I agreed. 'Will you fix it up, Heather?'

She looked at Julie, who nodded.

'Tell him to come over as soon as he can. And, Heather, be careful what you say on the telephone, won't you?'

Heather nodded and went out.

'What are you going to do, Mr Preston?

'Well, now that I know you'll be looked after, there's no point in my hanging around here. I have one or two other things to follow up. If I get lucky, I may come up on these guys from another direction.'

I got up to leave. She walked with me to the door, and I held out my hand.

'Mrs Van Dorn, thank you for what you're doing. If I said anything just now—'

'Forget it,' she interjected, shaking hands. 'You persuaded me against my better judgment, Mr Preston. You'd better make good.'

'I'll be trying,' I assured her. 'I'll call later to make certain Heather's boy friend is here, and to tell you what's happening.'

'Do,' she returned. 'Just because I'm calm now, it doesn't mean I shan't develop the jitters before long.'

'That I doubt.'

As I left the Alohah Apartments I tried to see whether I could spot anybody unusual hanging around. I knew it would be a waste of time. This was no amateur crowd I was bucking.

Instead of going back to the office I headed for Parkside Towers. It seemed obvious that if they didn't find whatever it was at Julie's place, they'd give my apartment the same treatment. Unlocking the door, I stepped inside. There was no shambles, at least not like that at the Van Dorn apartment. Here there was more evidence of method, and less destruction for its own sake. Almost without thinking I bent down to retrieve the telephone from the floor. When I straightened I found a man watching me.

'Mr Preston, isn't it? Time we had a little chat, sir.'

In his hand was a point three two automatic.

CHAPTER 9

Lots of people have the wrong idea about what a really dangerous man looks like. They conjure up in their heads a monstrous creature with an all-in wrestler's physique topped off by an ugly threatening face. The ugly face is essential, preferably emphasised by a blue shave and a flattened nose. The guy has usually long arms which make him seem to crouch as he walks, despite his impressive height. I have seen a few like that myself, a kind of composite man-ape-rogue elephant. But among the dangerous ones they are in the minority.

Take this character. He wasn't an inch above five four, and it was doubtful whether he tipped one hundred twenty pounds. He had flaxen hair, neatly brushed from a centre parting, and skin so pale it was almost translucent. He was wearing a faultless suit of charcoal grey, that didn't leave him car fare out of two hundred and fifty bucks. The striped silk tie was held in place by a stickpin, and stickpins being easy to lose, he had a pearl the size of a pea at one end to help him find it. He moved lightly on neat, small feet, and his hands were the artistic kind, with long tapering fingers like a violin player. To anybody else he might have looked like an undersized fairy, but to me he was different. This guy was murder on two legs.

'Shall we sit down, Mr Preston?' he asked politely. 'I always feel that two gentlemen like ourselves are more easy in their conversation if they are seated.'

I had strong doubts about how easy I was going to feel with this character under any circumstances. But he was the one with the artillery, so I sat. He nodded with satisfaction, and did the same, taking care not to disturb the knife edge crease in his pants.

'We're getting off to a fine beginning, sir, a splendid beginning. You haven't made any bother or asked a lot of pointless questions. Yes, I feel that you and I will get along splendidly.'

His voice was surprisingly deep and rich for such a small man, but there was something artificial about his delivery. He was careful with his diction as though it were something precious he'd acquired along the way, and not the natural habit of a lifetime.

'I always try to get along with people who point guns at me,' I informed him. 'Something to do with a life-wish.'

He smiled delightedly. It was obvious one of us was enjoying himself.

'Droll, sir. They told me you might not take me seriously.'

'Who did?' I asked quickly.

He shrugged in deprecation.

'Not so fast, Mr Preston. I am quite prepared to be open with you. Yes, I think I may say that. Open, sir. But we must not forget this, even when we are getting along so famously.'

He waved the gun airily. A thirty-two is not a very large weapon, but it can be a very deadly one in the right hands. Or the wrong hands, I should say. Looking at those slender and delicate fingers, I knew the gun was in a familiar grasp. I made a half bow.

'No, no, it won't do at all,' he went on. 'You ask questions, sir, a breach of taste in the circumstances, if you'll forgive my saying so. And you do not even offer anything in return.'

130

Now we were getting to the meat of the thing.

'What could I offer that might interest you?' I queried.

He chuckled, a quick dry sound.

'Ah, what indeed? Dreams, perhaps, a package of dreams?'

'Sorry, we're fresh out of dreams,' I replied.

A flicker of annoyance passed over his face, to be replaced at once by the bland smile.

'You're not thinking, Mr Preston. Not trying. Now, what could you think of that you have, that I might want?'

'You and plenty of other people, maybe,' I hazarded.

I hadn't the remotest idea what he was talking about, but I took a shot in the dark. Must have hit something too, judging by the momentary look of alarm the words evoked.

'What others, Mr Preston?' he asked softly.

It was my turn for the Buddha imitation. 'Just others.'

'Mr Preston,' he said at once, 'I must ask you not to trifle with me, please. A little humour, a little badinage, this is good between such as you and I. But I warn you, sir, I can become most uncertain-tempered if provoked.'

I could believe that. I must be careful not

to push this character too hard. But I thought he'd stand a little pushing still. If he'd been intending to kill me he would have done it at once. He wanted something, and he suspected I had it. Either that, or at least I knew where it was. I'd probably stay alive as long as he was without that information.

'You know what I can't figure?' I asked. 'You're looking for something, O.K. You make a search, like you have here. Things get untidy, but that's all. What makes no sense to me, is why a man like you should make such a pig-pen out of Mrs Van Dorn's apartment. She had one or two good pieces over there. Now they're ruined. I just don't see you doing that, but—?'

I shrugged and left the sentence floating in the air. He looked almost embarrassed.

'I need hardly say, I trust, that I did not conduct that little enquiry personally. I—er—contracted the work out, as they say. Nowadays one has to deal with terrible people on occasions. People quite unsuited to such delicate negotiations as these. Please assure the lady the damage is regretted.'

Truculently, I blared.

'And what about that other damage? To her face. Was that your employees' own idea, too?'

He held the gun more firmly, as though expecting me to charge at him at any second.

'No,' he replied crisply. 'That was a matter of business routine as I'm sure you well know. If the lovely Mrs Van Dorn had started involving the police in this matter, those huge boots would have been everywhere. I am not without some experience in these affairs, and believe me, interference from the police is seldom in the best interests of the principal parties involved.'

I nodded.

'Now you're making sense, No cops.'

Immediately his good humour was restored.

'Then it seems we are of one mind, on that score at least. Now, sir, shall we get down to the heart of the matter?'

'Why not? Mind if I smoke?'

'Er—please.'

As I went to put a hand in my pocket, he shook his head quickly and pointed the automatic at my middle. I froze.

'Smoke, by all means,' he continued. 'But honour me by smoking one of mine.'

Without taking his eyes off me, he slipped an elegant silver case from a side pocket, removed a cigarette and tossed it across. A small book of matches followed. I nodded my thanks and lit the cigarette. It was perfumed, naturally.

'Your good manners are really very highly developed for a man in your curious trade, Mr Preston. You haven't asked my name,' he pointed out.

'Would it do any good?'

He treated me to the dry chuckle again.

'I'll tell you,' he decided. 'It is Powell, Kingsland Powell. The name is perhaps familiar to you?'

I shook my head.

'I don't read much fiction.'

If I expected it to annoy him, I was disappointed. The tiny frame shook, this time with huge laughter.

'You really are a very amusing fellow, Mr Preston. And of course, you are absolutely right. My name is not Kingsland Powell at all. However, that is the name by which I am known at the moment, and I do not wish to confuse you by giving you any other.'

'O.K,' I said tiredly. 'Now we both know who you're not. What happens next?'

'Now I shall be more frank with you,' he said expansively. 'Oh, please, do not seem so sceptical. I assure you that frankness is my aim. At least, such a degree of frankness as will bring our business to a mutually satisfactory conclusion.'

I never met anybody who could do such a

lot of talking, and get so little said.

'You certainly took your time getting round to it,' I told him.

That didn't ruffle him in the least.

'True,' he nodded. 'But I've been sizing you up, to use the vernacular. Assessing you, if you prefer. I have decided we can do business. And now, the details. For one thing, I am aware that you are not really a principal in this affair, or more accurately, not *the* principal. I know the identity of the man you represent, and it is really he I should prefer to deal with. Unhappily he has permitted the distrustful element in his nature to persuade him to act as an absentee partner. In brief, sir, he is lying low.'

I always pride myself on a poker face, but this sharp-eyed little man must have detected something.

'Ah, I see I have made my point. Good, good. To proceed. Your—er—shall we say, employer, has something in his possession which is not his property. It is mine.'

'You say,' I contradicted. 'What makes it yours?'

'A figure of speech,' he corrected. 'You are quite right, of course. It is no more mine than yours. It is the property of certain interests whom I have the honour to represent.'

I chuckled.

'Why, Powell, you and me, we're just a couple of errand boys. We sit around here bluffing each other, while the real boys don't lift a finger.'

He looked pained.

'Please do not classify my principals under the same category as this worthless creature who hired you. I must ask you to believe, sir, that I speak for a group of financiers of international repute. Men of power, people of standing, who could do much, yes a great deal, for a man like yourself. What will you get from Nielson? Five hundred dollars, a thousand? Ah, I see I have your full attention.'

He had, at that. Not because of the bribe which was going to be offered any moment. What caught me off balance was the name Nielson. When Powell had started his spiel about the man who hired me, I'd assumed automatically he was talking about Frank Hawkins. Nielson was a new development, and I would have to watch my mouth for the rest of the interview. If Powell had any idea I didn't know what he was talking about, there was no telling what he might do.

'Your full attention,' he repeated almost absently-mindedly. 'Well, I do not criticise, oh, no, far from it. We are but base creatures, sir, all of us in this unhappy world. I think no less of a man for taking a natural interest in his own well-being.'

'Unless his well-being involves double-crossing somebody,' I contributed.

I'd intended that as an allusion to the bribe I was to get for selling out Nielson, whoever he might be. To my surprise, Powell's face darkened.

'Well said, Mr Preston, well said,' he breathed nastily. 'If Nielson had played the game with me, there would have been no necessity for all this tiresome tomfoolery. I'm compelled to say, it's a trifle disappointing to find a man of your obvious capabilities selling himself to a person like that.'

'What kind of person is he?' I ventured.

Powell looked at me suspiciously, uncertain whether I was trying to be funny.

'You mean you don't know?' he asked. 'Well, I think I believe you. I always like to think the best of people, and it would be more in keeping with my analysis of your character if you had been inveigled into the affair without knowing the full facts.'

'Very flattering,' I observed drily. 'Why don't you give me the facts, then you and I can decide what to do about Nielson?'

His face became crafty. With the barrel of

137

the thirty-two he tapped at the side of his nose.

'Ha ha,' he laughed quickly. 'I find this quite embarrassing. Really, quite embarrassing. If you hadn't previously realised your employer's part, how do I know what else he has kept from you? Forgive me if I sound blunt, sir, but I would not consider it fair trading for me to give you a lot of free information, in return for nothing. It goes against all good business principles.'

I nodded.

'Tell me one thing. Is it the stuff you really want, or is it Nielson?'

He smiled. Until he did that I'd been on the verge of forgetting the evil in this minature clothes horse who called himself Kingsland Powell. But there was a quality of unholy joy in the smile that reminded me, and sent a quick cold stab between my shoulder blades.

'Business must always take precedence over personal matters, Mr Preston. My purpose here, sir, is to recover the—er—ah—stuff, on behalf of its rightful owners. However, I should be less than human if I were to deny that I look forward to my next encounter with Mr Nielson, and with strong personal pleasure.'

I was glad my name wasn't Nielson.

'I wouldn't want to give an impression of

doubting your word, Mr Powell,' I mimicked his own speech pattern. 'But the ownership seems to be a matter of disagreement between yourself and certain other parties. There are two men for instance, brothers. They may have quite different views.'

He leaned forward with a serious expression.

'The gentlemen in question would perhaps own a store in this city?'

'They would,' I confirmed.

He became almost excited.

'I had not been informed that you were in contact with them. This is most unfortunate. I urge you, Mr Preston, to take care. These are evil men, men of violence and of inferior character quality. Believe me, I think only of your welfare. I had experience of this precious pair some years ago in another connection. They are not our sort, sir. Unpredictable men of low calibre. Totally untrustworthy. The—ah—merchandise is no more their property than Nielson's. And now, enough of this. I have enjoyed talking with you, but all good things must come to an end.'

He stood up quite suddenly, a rapid and smooth movement. Weighing the gun in his hand, he looked down at me thoughtfully. I hoped fervently the end he'd mentioned wasn't going to be mine, but I tried not to show it.

Powell gave that short bark of a laugh again.

'I will say you're a man not easily frightened, Mr Preston. That is a most useful characteristic for people engaged in the type of endeavour we now have under consideration. However, you need not concern yourself. I hold no grudge against you in any personal way whatever. Please accept that as the truth it is. I shall now make you an offer. I shall make it once only. The terms are not subject to amendment, so please do not attempt to haggle. I am prepared to pay you ten thousand dollars once the goods have been restored to me. That is the business for which I have been engaged. In addition I make you a personal offer of one thousand dollars of my own money, if you will put me in touch with Mr Nielson after our main business has been concluded.'

We live in a funny world where a man gets offered a thousand dollars for another man's life, and ten times that amount for some merchandise, all in one lovely package deal.

'I'll think about it,' I told him.

'Pray do, pray do. But not too long, please. I shall contact you this evening for a definite answer. No hedging, please, there will be no repeat offer. And now I really must be off.'

You'd have thought he was the vicar leaving after four o'clock tea in one of those British comedies. Only the gun struck a discordant note. He went to the door in brisk side-steps, neither his eyes nor the thirty-two leaving me for an instant.

'Hey,' I called. 'Suppose I tell Nielson about the personal offer? He might give me two thousand to put the finger on you instead.'

He nodded carefully.

'True. That is perfectly true. But consider, my dear sir, what on earth could you do with the money? You'd be in your grave.'

With a quick bow he let himself out. I made no attempt to follow him. Instead, I sat in the ruins and lit an Old Favourite. The perfume in that cigarette Powell had given me had left a bitter taste on my tongue. I felt a curious contentment. Finally, I was making progress. There is often a point during an investigation when you begin to feel you're not wasting your time. Especially when things begin to scuttle out of the woodwork. Things like the Elmans, Powell and now this new character Nielson. He was a man I was looking forward to meeting.

CHAPTER 10

There seems to be a tenancy regulation at the Parkside Towers that any time I want to take a shower the telephone has to ring. I don't know how the management achieve this. Maybe they have the plumbing connected to the telephone company exchange. Sometimes I try to play smart. I get stripped off, turn on the shower and wait, but it doesn't do any good. It isn't until I'm actually under that fine spray and beginning to enjoy it that the system operates. I'm getting used to it now, and sometimes I don't even use bad words when it happens. I stepped gingerly into the cold jets, shivered quickly, and began to soap up. It was great, it was fine. The phone rang. I said a bad word, groped around for a towel and padded off.

'Well?' I snarled.

'Preston? It's me, Hawkins. What'd you find out?'

'Oh, hello, just a minute.'

I set down the receiver, rubbed briefly here and there with the towel, fixed it more firmly round me and picked up the phone again.

'I don't know that I found out anything at all,' I told Hawkins.

'You're sure busy on it, I'll say that,' he observed. 'Four times already I called your office, and that woman told me you were out on a case. Hey,' he added suspiciously, 'I hope that's the same case?'

'Same one,' I assured him. 'As I say, I haven't come up with much. Can I try you with some names?'

'Go ahead,' he invited.

'Ever hear of a man named Kingsland Powell?'

He repeated it carefully.

'This is a man, or a company title?'

I told him it was a man.

'No,' he replied definitely. 'Got any more?'

'Nielson.'

'Lots of Nielsons,' he agreed. 'Plenty of Swedes at sea, you know. Got anything to go with it?'

I had to admit I hadn't.

'How about Augustin?' was my next try.

He sounded sceptical.

'What's it, a rib? The guy who got shot today? Naturally I heard of him.'

'Because he got shot, do you mean, or had you heard of him before?'

'Sure, I heard of him before today. Big

143

business name in town. You're not telling me a guy like that had anything to do with what happened to Jeff?'

'I'm not telling you anything,' I reminded him, 'I don't know anything. All I'm doing is to try on a few names for size. His widow says she knew Jeff.'

'Really?' he sounded pleased, 'Well, nice people always took to the boy. Where'd the old lady say she met him?'

'At the Oyster's Cloister. And she's not so very old,' I corrected.

Hawkins didn't seem to hear that part.

'See what I mean about the boy?' he demanded. 'That's the kind of connection could have done a lot for him. Imagine her remembering, eh?'

'Yes,' I said.

I didn't think it was an appropriate moment to tell my client the kind old lady was a man-eater. Instead, I asked,

'I didn't know you were a friend of the Elman brothers.'

'Oh that,' he agreed reluctantly. 'That's one of those things. You remember our deal? You dig your hole and I'll dig mine.'

'Just so we meet in the middle,' I cautioned.

'We will,' he stated. 'I had a kind of feeling you'd do something. Now I'm sure of it.'

'Why' I queried. 'I don't seem to be getting anywhere at all.'

Hawkins snorted.

'Not much you haven't. All you've got is a bunch of names I never even heard before. Including one rich widow who was a friend of Jeff's and I never knew it. You're going good, Preston, you'll turn something up.'

'Maybe, I'll be trying anyway,' I conceded. 'You have anything new you want to tell me?'

'No,' he denied. 'You're doing fine as you are. How's the dough situation, you need some more?'

'It's O.K. till now,' I replied. 'I'll let you know when it runs out. Where will I contact you?'

'Don't worry about it. I'll be in touch. Well, that's it I guess. So long.'

'So long.'

I stared thoughtfully at the instrument in my hand before resting it back in its cradle. My client had evidently not yet rid himself of this cloak and dagger idea about the two of us working independently. From what I'd seen of him, he was a man who could take care of himself if he had to. But if any one of the half-baked theories in my head proved to be close to the truth, he was going to find himself dealing with people who didn't go in for the old-style man-to-man bit. Man-to-four guys from behind was more their pattern, and tough as he may be, even Hawkins would not be able to laugh that off.

I was standing there thinking gloomy thoughts when the buzzer sounded. Absent-mindedly I wandered over to the door and opened it.

'Did you know I was coming, or have you got some other dame in there?'

Avis Augustin stood pointing at me. I'd forgotten I was only wearing a towel.

'Ah, the sorrowing widow,' I greeted. 'Are you coming in?'

She put a hand on her hip, stuck out the nearest half of her beautiful bust and said archly,

'Will I be safe?'

'With me, on a desert island,' I returned sourly, walking inside.

She followed me in and closed the door.

'Aren't we nasty this evening. Do I sit down?'

'Do as you please. I'm going to get dressed.'

For all my smart talk, I knew I wouldn't last ten minutes against this bundle of animal energy if she got an idea in her head. Charles Augustin may be a heel, but he was only heel-on-the-spot. Any man would have made the same mistake. Well, maybe not any man, but it would take a character of exceptionally strong will to spend any length of time in proximity to a natural primitive like Avis and not do something about her. I got dressed in record time and went back outside. She was sitting in a low chair and her already short skirt was hiked well above the knees. She might as well still be in a bathing suit. In her hand was a glass and she raised it in mock ceremony.

'You said to do as I pleased,' she reminded me.

'Help yourself. What do you want, anyway?'

I sat well away from her and pushed an Old Favourite in my mouth. She pouted.

'You don't go in much for the big host routine, do you?' she asked.

'With guests only. You just walked in,' I reminded her. 'What's it all about?'

She looked at me curiously, as though unable to be persuaded that she really had that little impact on me. I looked back stonily as though she had.

'You're a cold fish,' she told me. 'All right. I'll tell you why I'm here. I want you to make them let Charles go.'

'Make who let him go where?'

'The police,' she said snappily. 'Make them let him out of jail.'

'Jail?' I repeated, as though it hadn't quite sunk in. It hadn't. 'Why would they put him in jail?'

'They say he murdered his father. My husband,' she added defiantly.

I made a face and pulled on the cigarette. This was a development I had not considered possible.

'Well?' she demanded.

'Well?' I replied irritatingly.

'Well get down there and tell 'em to let him out,' she demanded.

I grinned.

'Oh, sure. They love that, down at headquarters. They sit there trembling, waiting for some nosy P.I to stick his head in and shout, 'I demand the release of this man.' You must think I'm crazy. The best I could hope for would be to get tossed out on my can. I'd be lucky if somebody didn't wrap a nightstick round my head.'

She shook her head impatiently. This caused some interesting jouncing movements under the tight black blouse.

'They'll listen to you, they have to. You were there, you know he didn't do it.'

I shook my head, but couldn't compete with the rest of the movement.

'I was there, yes, but I don't know anything of the kind.'

Avis stared in genuine astonishment.

'But you were there. Charles told me you'd

seen us, seen what we were doing before we knew you'd arrived.'

'So?'

'So you know he couldn't have done it. How could anybody kill someone and then—and then—'

'I have the message,' I told her.

'All right then, how can you possibly think Charles could have done it?'

'I don't think anything of the kind,' I assured her.

'Then I don't see why—' she began.

'Because what I think doesn't matter,' I explained. 'What matters is what the police think, and if they think Charles, that's it.'

She curled her lip, and it wasn't attractive.

'Cops,' she sneered. 'Don't tell me about cops. They're always on the prowl for somebody they can push around. They don't care about innocent people or guilty people. All they want is to get their dirty hands on somebody, anybody, and start waling into them—I know cops.'

I held up a finger.

'Correction,' I said. 'You know some cops, and the wrong ones, by the sound of it. Most of them are not that way at all. And certainly not Rourke. If Rourke says it's Charles, he has good reasons.'

All the same, I wasn't easy about it. On the few facts I knew I couldn't put the killing of Albert F Augustin down to his son's account. Rourke would have good reasons all right, but I'd give a lot to know what they were.

Avis said in disbelief,

'You're going to let them keep him in there, without so much as lifting your little finger?'

'I didn't say that,' I pointed out. 'Not that any of this is my business, but I'll take a ride round there and find out what gives.'

She sighed with relief.

'Well, that's better. I figured you couldn't be all stone. I'll come with you.'

'No you won't,' I contradicted. 'You'll scram out of here and let me know where I can get in touch with you. If the son of Albert F Augustin is being held for his murder, the station will be crawling with press people. One look at you in that outfit is all they'll need. They'll smear you good for the morning editions. Where will you be?'

She made a face.

'In a bar.'

'What bar?' I insisted.

'Any bar, all the bars. Who cares? This is the first real night I've had free from that mausoleum, and brother I'm not going to waste it.'

I got up.

'Go to Sam's,' I ordered. 'You know it?'

She nodded.

'Used to go there quite a bit one time.'

'All right. Sam's a friend of mine. You tell him I'll be calling you there, and he'll see you're not bothered.'

'I might want to be bothered.'

'Not until this is straightened out,' I ordered. 'Look, you want me in this, all right I'm in it. But until I find out what's going on, you are going to behave yourself. Or I'll leave him in there, so help me.'

She studied me carefully to see whether I meant it. I meant it.

'O.K,' she said resignedly. 'Just don't be too long.'

I walked with her to the door. As I went to open it, she turned quickly, pressing herself against me, nails at the nape of my neck forcing my head down to the parted red lips. Then she wasn't forcing me at all, and I was still crushing her against me. Suddenly she pushed me away and laughed up in my face mockingly.

'I thought so,' she scoffed. 'A bluffer.'

I was breathing heavily.

'You're a bitch,' I told her hoarsely.

She laughed again and opened the door.

'So what else is new? Don't leave it too long.'

I stared at the closed door for a full minute after she'd left. I was angry with myself for what had happened. Angry, and other things all mixed together. Somewhere in there was a hint of despair, too. Because I knew what she was, what she'd always been. Knew what she must have done to Charles Augustin and who knows how many others. Knew too, that it would probably happen again, if she wanted it to.

When I left the apartment I was in an evil frame of mind.

CHAPTER 11

The sun was low on the horizon and throwing deep orange splashes on to the sombre facade of the Monkton City P.D Headquarters building. They looked like giant blood spots, or maybe it was just the way I was feeling at the time. The man at the desk told me it was all right to go on up, so I tramped the weary flights leading to the sumptuous accommodation occupied by the homicide boys.

Rourke barked bad-temperedly at my knock,

gave a second growl when he saw who it was coming in.

'What do you want?' he barked.

I put my right hand on my left shoulder.

'Somebody from the *po*—lice told me to get down here and sign something.'

'Oh,' he muttered. 'Oh, yeah. Yeah. Schultz, take this man's statement.'

Schultz pulled a pad of forms to the centre of Randall's desk and motioned me to sit down.

'Tell me you made sergeant, Schultzie,' I said.

'It was me told you,' he reminded. 'And I didn't really make anything, not yet. I'm keeping the stripes warm till Gil Randall gets well. That's all.'

'Never mind the chit-chat, sergeant,' bawled Rourke. 'Just take his statement and throw him out. We have more to do around here than sit chinning it up with a fancy pants private policeman.'

Schultz said no more, but started filling in some of the blank spaces at the top of the pad. Then we did the question and answer bit, which somehow miraculously produces a coherent statement at the end. We'd both had lots of practice, and twenty minutes later it was done. Schultz passed it over for me to read.

153

'I want to see that, sergeant,' Rourke interrupted.

The temporary sergeant walked across and dumped it in front of his irascible boss. Rourke read it carefully, then again.

'Either you have a very good memory, or you were telling the truth this afternoon,' he admitted grudgingly.

'There's no "either" about it,' I assured him. 'I have an excellent memory, *and* I was telling you the truth this afternoon.'

'Huh.'

'You want me to wait till it's typed up, or could I sign later?' I queried.

Rourke put on his long-suffering patient servant of the public expression.

'Wait?' he asked softly. 'No, we wouldn't want to put you to that inconvenience, Mr Preston. After all, it's nothing but a leading statement in a little old death-by-shooting incident. You must have a million more important things to do, like hitting a few bars for instance. We won't detain you, sir. I'll have this silly old thing ready by tomorrow, then the mayor will bring it round to your home for signature. Will that be convenient?'

Rourke has many moods, and this heavy-handed sarcasm is one of his most dangerous. But I wanted to know about Charles Augustin.

'About Augustin—' I began. It was as far as I got.

'Get out. Out.'

Rourke's heavy fist crashed on the desk. Schultz winked briefly, grabbed me by the shoulder and opened the door.

'I'll toss this guy out, lieutenant,' he promised.

Out in the corridor he let go of me and grinned apologetically.

'Sorry about that, Preston. Way the old man's feeling he'd have charged you with something if I hadn't dragged you out.'

I nodded my thanks.

'I believe he would. I haven't seen him so evil in months. What happened?'

Schultz walked along beside me as I made my way downstairs.

'You know the lieutenant, he's a lawman. He hates politicians and people who pull strings. Specially when he has to dance on the end of one. Well, he pulled a boner today. He detained Charles Augustin.'

'I was going to ask him about that. What made him do it? I thought he was convinced the guy was in the clear?'

Schultz motioned me to be quiet, and didn't speak again until we were standing outside the building.

'You were right when you said Augustin was in the clear,' he admitted. 'But only of killing the old man. He caused us a hell of a lot of trouble.'

'In what way?'

The policeman stared at the setting sun. 'That's what they can't really capture, you know. Can't really get it on the canvas. Look at the different reds and browns that sun is striking over there. And that kind of grey-red where it's hitting those clouds. They get some beautiful effects, but they never really hit it, do you think?'

'I didn't know you were interested in painting, Schultzie,' I said. 'But I see what you mean.'

He laughed quickly.

'Just interested, that's all. And I'm glad that's all. A man could spend his whole life trying to do just that one thing, and never quite make it. I don't think I'd like that. Anyway, where was I?'

'About Augustin wasting your time,' I prompted.

'Oh—yes. Well, you know what the setup was when we got there. Big murder mystery, no weapon, and all the rest of it. Rourke and me spent a couple of hours searching around and racking our brains for a reasonable explanation. Augustin's daughter was there by then, a Mrs Chappel.'

'Martha Chappel?' I queried.

'Yes, do you know her?'

'No, but Charles told me his sister's name was Martha, I didn't know her other name.'

'Oh. Well, she and this Charles spent a lot of time talking and arguing. Finally, she practically dragged him to Rourke and I, and said he'd got something to tell us. Boy, she wasn't kidding.'

He stopped for a moment, but not for dramatic effect. He was thinking back to the scene at the Augustin house, and without much pleasure.

'You know what he'd done, that nitwit? He could see his father had shot himself, when he first found the body. The gun was still in the old man's hand. So he took it, sent you into the house, and hid it in the swimming pool. It was under the low diving board.'

I digested this slowly.

'What made him do a crazy thing like that?' I asked.

Schultz shrugged.

'Who knows. He gave us a dozen reasons. He couldn't bear anybody to know the old man was a suicide. He couldn't face the possibility it might have been partly his fault, because of

157

the thing between him and the old man's wife. He was afraid the business interests might be adversely affected if the suicide story got out. He was afraid the wife might have done it and planted the gun in the old man's hand, and he wanted to protect her.'

He took a deep breath.

'He had other reasons. They were all mixed up together and they came pouring out like beans out of a can. Maybe the truth is, he just did it on impulse, and the reasons sort of got added in later.'

'I see. No wonder Rourke was so touchy just now.'

'That's not the reason,' Schultz contradicted. 'Oh, he was mad, all right. I can tell you, that man was sizzling when he heard Augustin's story. He said to me, "Schultz, we're going to teach this guy a lesson. We're going to teach him he can't fool around with the police department this way." '

'So he took him in,' I commented.

'Yeah. How did you know?' said the detective in a surprised tone.

'I heard about it. Then what happened?'

'Well, we got Augustin down here to headquarters, and took a statement. Then we questioned him for an hour or so, then we took another statement. After that we had two other guys grill him for an hour, then they took a statement. We didn't do a thing to harm him, just wanted him to remember not to fool around like that another time.'

I knew the procedure, knew the soul-destroying experience of the endless, seemingly pointless questions, the insistent hammering at trivial details. Not that I felt any sympathy for Charles Augustin. That had been a stupid trick for a grown man of his intelligence, and if I had any sympathies these were with Rourke. This time.

'The lieutenant and me took the next shift,' Schultz continued. 'By that time the guy was beginning to get the idea it don't pay to interfere with police business. Then there was all hell. The sister, this Mrs Chappel, she turned up here with just about everybody in town who had any right to call himself a lawyer. They really tore into us. Then the Chief sent for the old man. When he came back, he was so mad I was afraid he might kill somebody. I never saw a man so angry. So the Augustin guy walked out, and that about brings you up to date.'

I said,

'Thanks. You probably did do me a favour when you removed me from the Rourke orbit. One I owe you.'

'I'd better get back upstairs. When he's like he is now, I feel safer where I can watch him all the time.'

Schultz nodded and went inside. I stood for a moment, thinking. There were several things I had to do and it was already after eight o'clock. I found a phone in the joint across the street where the department boys drop in for coffee. When I got through, a man answered. I didn't hang up.

'Mrs Van Dorn, is she there, please?' I queried.

'Who is this?'

The man's voice was guarded, suspicious.

'Tell her it's Preston.'

'Mr Preston, the detective?' he asked.

'Correct.'

'I'm Jack Wells,' he told me. 'Say, I don't get all this cops and robbers bit. Seems to me if there's any chance of these ladies being in some kind of danger, we ought to call the police.'

And of course, he was quite right.

'I think that's up to them, don't you?' I replied. 'More particularly, it's up to Mrs Van Dorn. Nobody's threatening Heather, and nobody's forcing her to stay.'

'Look, I don't know what kind of pitch you gave them, but this is me you're talking to

160

now,' he said aggressively, 'And I'm telling you I think this stinks.'

One thing I didn't want was for him to walk out.

'Listen,' I said placatingly. 'I know it's unusual, but believe me there's something big here, and this is the best way to break it.'

'Way I hear it, it's these girls are going to get broken,' he retorted. 'And if they do, brother, you and me are going to have a little talk.'

'I'll try to get over to the apartment later tonight,' I suggested. 'Maybe I can explain it a little better.'

'I hope so. You want Mrs Van Dorn?'

'Tell her it won't take a minute.'

A few seconds later she picked up the 'phone.

'How long is all this going to take?' she demanded. 'I'm not going to spend my whole life cooped up like a—like a—'

'Take it easy,' I soothed. 'Anything happened? Any mail, any telephone calls?'

'Nothing. Not a damned thing. You do realise it's eight o'clock on a fine warm evening and I'm stuck here twiddling my thumbs.'

'I do, and I'm sorry about it,' I assured her. 'Believe me, I think it's for the best.'

She snorted.

'I'm sure that's supposed to be comforting. Forgive me if I don't see how. Jack said you might come over later. What for?'

Certainly not for the friendly reception I was going to get, I reflected.

'Well, now, Mrs Van Dorn, it seems to me you're doing quite a bit to help with something which is really none of your concern. It also seems to me the least I can do, to come and tell you what's happening.'

'Is something happening?' In her curiosity, she forgot to sound irritable.

'Quite a few things,' I hinted mysteriously. 'Tell you about them when I see you.'

Next I dialled my answering service and learned that Sam Thompson had called twice in the past hour. He would keep trying. I asked for the calls to be switched to my apartment and hung up.

I'd promised not to leave Avis too long, but it was more important I should hear what Sam Thompson had to say. Ten minutes later I pulled up outside Parkside Towers. When I entered the building, there was Sam hunched in a chair by the night man's desk.

'Well, well,' he scoffed. 'You do live here, then.'

'I told you to keep calling till you reached me,' I reminded.

'Keep calling,' he grumbled, slouching beside me to the elevator. 'I should spend all my money for the telephone company's benefit.'

I felt a momentary uneasiness entering the apartment, and realised I was half-expecting to find the man who called himself Kingsland Powell waiting for me. Sam watched me curiously.

'Expecting some beautiful dame to be standing in here with her tongue hanging out?' he asked.

'She'll be here one night,' I evaded. 'I don't want to miss her. Anyway, sit down, Sam, rest your feet.'

'I don't need to sit down,' he grunted. 'It's not my feet have been getting all the action. It's where I sit down that needs the rest.'

I grinned.

'Not much excitement, huh? Well, get yourself a drink. That usually helps whatever aches.'

He seemed to agree, judging by the speed with which he moved in on the bottles. He took a long pull at his drink, beamed with appreciation and sat down heavily.

'Ouch, I forgot,' he grumbled.

'Stop complaining, and let's hear what you found out,' I suggested.

He emptied the glass, smacked his lips and said,

'What was there to find out? If you were looking for the clean all-American girl, I found her. Her name is Susan Hofmeyer. Outside of that, nothing.'

'So tell me the nothing,' I insisted. 'After all it is my money.'

'True,' he shrugged. 'Here it is. The Hofmeyers are an old family hereabouts. They have a solid reputation for quiet living, paying their bills, keeping out of trouble. They are Mr and Mrs Main Street, and I do not kid you. Susan is the daughter, a beauty if you like 'em that young. She has this job at the delicatessen. Every morning she starts at eight-thirty, takes her lunch in the place, finishes at five in the afternoon. She is polite to the customers, reliable, a quick worker. Everybody has a high regard for Susan. She had a boy friend, but the kid was killed in an automobile smash a few months back. It didn't exactly break her heart, because now she has a new one. When she left work she caught the cross-town bus. I followed her to make sure she was going home. She wasn't. She stayed on the bus to the end of the line, about five miles out of town. There was a boy waiting for her. Just the boy you'd have expected. A nice-looking clean sort of boy, a garage hand still in his overalls. They hadn't got a bottle of rum, neither of them was carrying a gun. They weren't dressed like street corner hoodlums, and you know something else? They held hands. I tell you, Preston, following Susan Hoymeyer and winding up the day seeing her with that boy was a cleansing experience. With the kind of action you and I get used to around this neon sewer, it's hard to remember there are young people like that.'

Sam Thompson usually spoke in grunts, with an occasional sentence of ten words when it was forced from him. His account of the day's activity was little short of lyrical, by his standards. And Thompson for all his laziness was a particularly shrewd observer.

'Sounds as though our Susan got through to you, Sam.'

'True,' he agreed. 'That is true. I tell you, it almost made me sad. If I'd met a girl like that years ago, things would have been different.'

'Stop kidding yourself and have another drink,' I told him. 'You probably knew a dozen girls like that, and you backed off. No woman would stand for your idleness, and you know it.'

He looked aggrieved, but not so badly that

he'd refuse the offer of more of my liquor.

'Look, Preston, don't turn nasty, and spoil my day,' he begged. 'You're just sore because I didn't catch the girl planning a big jewel robbery or something. That's hardly my fault.'

He wasn't completely wrong. I didn't know what I'd been hoping for when I had him watch the Hofmeyer girl. It was just one of those long shots and it didn't pay off.

'How about those expenses?' I asked.

'Nothing to it,' he replied. 'Five'll be plenty.'

I handed over the bill and said,

'Sam, I hate to be a poor host, but I have to go out right away.'

'Right.'

He finished the drink in one swallow and made for the door.

'I'm going to spend the whole evening moping over my wasted life,' he told me. 'Next time you have a tail-job, make it somebody a little more unsavoury, will you?'

'I'll try.'

I gave him a couple of minutes to get clear, then went back downstairs. I opened the door of the Chev and climbed in. From behind, somebody said,

'Just drive away nice and easy, and there won't be no trouble.'

I'd have felt more comforted by the words if there hadn't been the cold feeling of a ring of metal at the nape of my neck.

CHAPTER 12

'Where are we going?' I asked.

'Just drive,' suggested my passenger. 'I'll tell you the moves.'

I rolled through the darkening streets, feeling helpless. Whoever this character was behind me he was no beginner. The beginner always sits next to the driver waving the gun about. A quick swerve at a corner and he is off-balance, and that gives the driver at least an even chance. But when the man with the gun is behind, the driver does as he's told.

'What's it all about?'

I hoped it sounded nonchalant.

'We just want a little talk, that's all,' he replied.

'So talk. I'm at your disposal.'

'I know that,' he snapped. 'You're going to stay that way if you want to keep all in one piece. Go left on Twelfth.'

I did as he said. I couldn't make out his face

in the rear mirror but the voice was familiar. With quiet excitement I realised this was one of the men who'd stuck those steel cutters in my mouth the night before. There'd been three of them that time, and no doubt the other two would be waiting wherever he was taking me. It wasn't a cheerful prospect, but at least something was moving.

'Turn off here.'

We were down in the Harbour area now, a run-down neighbourhood of abandoned stores and empty warehouses. I turned into a narrow street.

'Hold it.'

I braked.

'All right, out.'

I climbed out. The rear door opened immediately and my new friend was standing waiting as I swung the car door shut.

'You got a gun?' he demanded.

'It's in the car,' I replied.

'Maybe. Stand against the wall. And if you want to get dead, start something.'

He told me to lean against the wall on my upstretched hands, facing it. A hand slapped me here, there, expertly.

'All right, you're clean. But let me—'

The words tailed away in a strangled sob. There was a soft thud. A man said,

'How do you get in fixes like this, Preston?'

I turned around to see Sam Thompson standing over the prostrate figure of my late adversary.

'How'd you get here?' I whispered.

'Car wouldn't start. I was fooling around with the starter when I saw this character climb in the back of your Chev. I didn't know whether you'd think that was a good idea, so I kind of tagged along.'

'Nice tagging,' I complimented.

Assuming there were three of them, there were still two to be accounted for. Bending down I studied the face of the man on the ground. He was a stranger to me, though the type was familiar enough. A brawn and muscle character, not too strong on the think. Stripping off his tie I yanked his hands behind his back and tied them together. A soiled handkerchief I found in an inner pocket and with this I made a makeshift gag. A quick search of his clothes produced nothing that would give me a clue to who he was or why he should be interested in me. The gun was an Italian army weapon, a nine millimetre job. As I rose I handed it to Thompson.

'What now?' he asked suspiciously.

'This guy has friends,' I replied. 'They're

expecting me, and I'd hate them to be disappointed.'

Thompson looked apprehensively at the gun in his hand.

'The friends of a man who carries a thing like this in his pocket, them I don't want to see,' he protested. 'I'm too young to die.'

'Nobody's going to die,' I assured him. 'Those guys want to talk, and I feel like obliging. You want to go home, go home.'

'We-ell,' hedged Sam. 'I come this far so I guess I'll stick around.'

I didn't wait for him to change his mind. Opening the car door, I leaned inside and removed the .38 from the glove compartment.

'Nobody's going to die, huh?' sniffed Thompson.

'This is just to ensure nobody does. C'mon.'

There was a door ten feet away from where I'd parked. The warehouse I knew was not used, but the hinges swung smoothly as I pressed gently at the rotting wood. Somebody had been busy with an oil-can. I stepped inside, into darkness. Behind me, Thompson pulled the door shut. That way we didn't make a target in silhouette. I put my hand on Sam's arm to stay where he was. We both stood there a full two minutes, letting our eyes adjust to the darkness. The black became dark grey, and

170

then lighter. By straining, I found I could see several feet in front of me. A jab in the ribs and I turned to see Thompson pointing towards the roof. A tiny crack of light filtered from a closed door thirty feet from the ground.

'That's us, Sam,' I whispered.

We crept around the walls feeling each step carefully. This was no time to be stepping into a sudden hole and breaking a leg. After about ten minutes of this we came to the stairs, or more accurately, a rusting iron ladder. I went up carefully testing for safety and noise at each tread. It was a weird experience being able to see neither up nor down for any distance. Finally we made the top, a narrow catwalk that seemed to afford the only access to the one-time offices on our right. The chink of light came from the third door along. When I reached it I stood quite still, hardly daring to breathe, listening hard for any sound from inside. There was nothing. Thompson froze too, and we made faces at each other to indicate we couldn't hear anything. I waved the .38 and pointed it at the room. He shrugged, nodded and stood ready.

I went in low, turning the door knob and pushing forward violently, and at the same time bending double. Two men looked in startled surprise from the table where they sat. One dived a hand towards his shoulder.

'Don't,' I advised. 'I'll have to kill you, Georgie.'

He arrested the movement, staring his hate. The other man sat quite still, sizing up the situation. They both looked twice when Sam Thompson appeared behind me.

'You seem to know us,' said the calm one.

'I know you,' I confirmed. 'You're the Elmans. You're Cy, the one I talk to. The one with the eyeglasses is Georgie. You know the Elmans, Sam?'

'No,' he denied. 'My pleasure.'

'It's no pleasure,' I corrected. 'And watch Georgie. Cy is the one with whatever brains these two have, but Georgie's the one you watch. He has the mentality of a three-year-old, and he ought to be in a home. He's crazy, especially about hurting people.'

'You I'm gonna kill,' announced Georgie hoarsely.

'See what I mean, Sam?'

Cy still hadn't moved from the position he'd been in when I opened the door.

'Who are you, friend, and what do you want?' he asked quietly.

The table was busy with playing cards. That was why we'd heard nothing. Cy had been playing solitaire. I pulled up a spare chair and invited myself to the table, nodding to Thompson to stay where he was. He lounged at the doorway, watchful.

'We all know who I am, even the moron here, so let's stop playing games,' I suggested.

'Honest, Cy, you gotta stop him or I'm gonna take him, guns or not,' pleaded Georgie.

As he became worked up, the thick pebble glasses got steamy. He wasn't altogether attractive. Cy stopped fencing.

'What happened to Joe?' he enquired.

'Was that the ape you sent to collect me?' I guessed. 'He didn't tell me his name. You don't seem to do very well for help, do you? He told me you wanted to talk. So talk.'

'All right.'

He reached across and laid a nine of spades beneath a ten of hearts.

'Suddenly you turn up. You poke your nose in things which are none of your business. Why?'

'What things, Cy old pal? Tell me about the things,' I suggested.

'You been asking questions, bothering people, making noises. It can be unhealthy. Why?'

'You don't have much conversation, do you? And you seem to overlook this.'

I waved the .38 at him. He stared at it briefly.

'It's a gun,' he remarked casually. 'I've seen them before. Sometimes they frighten me. This isn't one of the times. You know what I think, Preston? I think you made a big mistake. You're messing in things you don't understand, and you don't know how to stop. Take a tip, if you don't want a cut-price funeral. Stay out of this.'

I shook my head.

'Too late for that, Elman. There's money here. Big money. I want mine.'

'What you'll get is a bullet right between the eyes,' promised Georgie throatily.

I'd thought so before, and now I was positive. Georgie was the one who'd spoken to me while those steel cutters were inside my mouth the night before.

'You gave me a friendly warning last night, didn't you, crazy boy? That was you who wanted to cut my tongue out.'

He giggled nervously. It was repulsive.

'What is this money you're talking about?' asked Cy warily.

'Just money. I probably wouldn't have known if it hadn't been for Nielson.'

'Nielson?' queried Georgie. 'You mean—?'

'Shut up, George,' cut in his brother swiftly. 'I'll talk to the man. You were saying about Nielson?'

'Nothing about him. By the way there's a friend of yours in town. Kingsland Powell.'

'Never heard of him,' replied Cy.

It wasn't the words I believed. It was the expression of vacant surprise on Georgie's face.

'He changes his name a lot,' I said.

I described Powell. This time Georgie's face wasn't so empty.

'Say, Cy, you don't suppose—'

'Will you shut up and let me handle this,' demanded Cy.

'Look, Preston, you had a tip last night. You're very lucky. Guys who interfere with my business don't usually get any warning at all. You're getting two. Keep out of it. It's too big for a cheap shamus to handle.'

I laughed.

'Really. But it's O.K for you and the lunatic here?'

That was too much for Georgie. With a choking cry he lunged at me across the table. I swayed back from the grasping hands, as they crashed to the table. Then I swung the .38 hard down on his right wrist. He screamed with agony as the heavy metal crunched into bone and sinew. Cy jumped up but Thompson was there pointing the machine pistol at his head. Georgie fell back in his chair, sobbing and nursing the broken hand.

'You're through now, Preston,' promised Cy. 'You're as good as dead.'

'Not quite,' I contradicted.

I got up and went to the crumpled figure of his brother. Reaching inside his coat I pulled out a heavy .45 revolver.

'See if he's got one, Sam,' I jerked a thumb at Cy Elman.

Thompson frisked the silent man.

'Nothing,' he reported.

'Well, thanks for the talk. I won't be seeing you guys for a long time.'

'That's what you think. You'll be dead inside twenty-four hours,' threatened Cy.

'Maybe. But it won't be your doing.'

I pulled Georgie's glasses off and tapped at each lens with the automatic.

'Let's go, Sam.'

Sam had been puzzled at the trick with the glasses, but he said nothing. As we walked out Cy Elman stood and watched silently. We made quick time down the iron stairway and back out to the street. The third man, Joe, was twisting about on the ground trying to free his hands. I knelt down and held the .38 at his face. He went very still.

'Joe, you're in trouble with Cy and Georgie. They want you upstairs. Get up.'

I grasped him by the shoulder and heaved him upright.

'I told Georgie you double-crossed him and Cy, and let me and my friend in there with guns. Georgie didn't like that.'

Joe couldn't say anything because of the gag, but a thin rivulet of sweat coursed suddenly down his forehead.

'I'm giving you a break, Joe,' I went on. 'You can beat it. Just as you are. Or else you can stay here and wait for Georgie to come down.'

He shook his head with rapid fear. I looked at my watch.

'He'll be down in about five minutes. You staying?'

Again he shook his head. He didn't really believe I was going to turn him loose.

'You heard the man,' barked Thompson. 'Scram.'

Joe glanced uncertainly from one of us to the other. Then slowly he turned and took a step. Finding that we weren't kidding, he broke into an awkward shambling trot and soon disappeared. Thompson wasn't impressed with me at the moment.

'What was all that about up there just now?' he demanded.

'Nothing much,' I admitted. 'I don't know

177

any more than when we started. I was hoping those two might tell me something, and I'm sure Georgie would have, but the other one wasn't going to be bluffed.'

'Well, I may as well tell you right now,' said Thompson disgustedly. 'That was a pretty cheap trick, breaking the guy's glasses. Like somebody kicking a blind man.'

'Steady on Sam. I did that for a special reason. You know how hard it is to find your way down that stairway in the dark. With no glasses, Georgie won't dare try. He's pinned up there either till daylight, or until his brother can get a spare pair to him.'

'Oh.' Thompson mellowed considerably. 'Yes, that makes some sense. But so what? Who needs him trapped up there?'

'We do. Follow me and you'll see why.'

I climbed into the Chev while he went back to his own car. I backed out of the narrow street and headed across town, Thompson's lights on my tail. After a few blocks I pulled in outside a drug-store. Thompson followed me inside, still mystified. At the counter I made change, then headed for the phone.

'Police Headquarters,' said a bored voice.

'Gimme the Fraud Squad, Sergeant Brooks.'

Click, click.

'Brooks. Who is this?'

'Preston,' I told him. 'Vince, you're interested in the Elmans, I think you said?'

'I'm interested all right,' he confirmed.

'Well, it's not a fraud case, but they broke into a warehouse tonight. They're still there.'

Behind me Thompson said, 'Ah.'

'What's the address?' snapped Brooks.

'The old Muller and Fielding Company place. Crane Street.'

'How can you be sure they're still around?' he queried.

'I'm sure,' I said flatly. 'Do you want 'em or not?'

'I want 'em. Thanks, Preston.'

I hung up, and grinned at Thompson.

'Now it's clear?'

'Now it's clear,' he agreed. 'I'm sorry for thinking what I did.

'Forget it. At least those two are out of my hair for a while. Let's go get a drink.'

'I'm with you,' he assented. 'Where we going?'

'Sam's place.'

He screwed up his face.

'That's a joke? You know everybody always asks if I own the joint.'

'Sorry, Sam. Has to be. There's someone there waiting for me.'

At least, I hoped so. Avis Augustin had

enough of a start on me to have collected at least a dozen guys by this time. And she was a girl unlikely to be put off by quantity.

CHAPTER 13

Sam's was busy. It was nine-thirty of a warm evening, and half the people in town had decided that there was the only place to take a thirst. With difficulty, and a lot of neat elbow-work, I made my way to the bar. Sam was busy, pouring out drinks of every description as fast as his fingers could work. Finally, I caught his eye.

'I sent a friend here, Sam, a lady. Is she here?'

He looked at me with despair, then rolled his eyes towards the packed and milling crowds.

'Mr Preston, I couldn't tell ya if Elizabeth Taylor was in here, now could I?'

'This was about three hours ago,' I pressed. 'A blonde, plenty of everything.'

'Oh that one,' he nodded. 'Yeah, her I remember. The place was half-empty then. Sure, she was here. Didn't stay though. You wanta drink?'

'Scotch on the rocks. Mansize. Make it two.'

When he came back I passed him a bill, waited for change.

'Did she just walk out, or did somebody call for her? It's important, Sam.'

'I don't know. When I get a chance I'll ask Ed if he noticed anything.'

It didn't matter. It couldn't matter. Avis Augustin had thought better of it. She had more to do with her life than sit around in bars all alone. She probably decided I wasn't going to show and took off.

'What are you worrying about?'

Thompson's bored voice suddenly reminded me where I was.

'Worried? Who's worried?'

'You are.' He made it a statement. 'There's plenty more blondes.'

'Not like this one,' I assured him.

But he was right. I was worried, even though I couldn't think of any logical reason why I should be.

'Mr Preston?'

Sam's voice came through the din, I leaned close to him as he inclined his head across the counter.

'Ed remembers your friend. Who wouldn't? He says she stayed about half an hour then up and walked out. Ed was watching her most of the time, and if you knew Ed you'd believe it. He says he don't remember anybody talking to her.'

'Thanks, Sam. I'm obliged.'

I had to see Avis. It made no sense, and I knew it, but some sense told me I had to see her and talk to her. I wanted to know she was all right. It was ridiculous. What could happen to her? Why should anything happen to her? I was just being spooky. What I needed was to stay right where I was and have another drink.

'I'm leaving, Sam. Stick around if you want.'

'If you're sure nobody's going to hold you up again,' he observed drily. 'I might as well stick here and sample the crops.'

I nodded and elbowed my way back out to the dark street. Soon I was heading out of town in the direction of Lake Minaho and the Augustin home. About eight miles along the highway I suddenly caught the mournful wail of a siren, and in the centre of the rear mirror a large white blob told me there was a motor-cycle patrolman on my tail. I checked the gauge, and saw the needle flickering on the fifty reading. Not that it would do me any good, I knew. If this man was behind with his monthly quota of speeding raps, I was doing sixty-five, and the best thing to do was grin.

As he drew alongside he waved a gauntleted hand, and headed me into the side of the road. I pulled up and waited. He got off and walked towards me, unbuttoning the flap on his revolver holster. Maybe a bank had been blown up or something.

'Your name Preston?' he demanded, peering in suspiciously.

To say I was taken aback was putting it mildly.

'It is,' I confirmed. 'What's it all about?'

'Don't ask me. County Sheriff wants you. Let's go.'

'Wait a minute,' I protested. 'I have a right to know what's going on. You can't just stop people on the open highway and drag 'em away like this.'

He sighed.

'Look, mister, I just do what I'm told. You're on the air, you and this car. Don't let's have a lot of argument. Just turn around and start driving.'

I wasn't going to make any progress with this guy. With a curse I started up, and wheeled round in a wide circle. He got back astride his machine and buzzed up beside me.

'You go in front. And no funny business.'

I said something he couldn't hear above the growling motor and moved back towards

Monkton. He kept steadily a few feet behind all the way. After about three minutes he accelerated and came alongside, pointing up ahead. That was when I forgot how annoyed I was, and felt only interest. He was pointing to a huge illuminated sign that announced the Beano Club was one half-mile further along the road. I nodded to let him know I understood, and a few seconds later I slowed down to make the turn into the curving drive. When I'd called at the club that morning it had ben practically deserted. Now I noticed the lines of cars in the forecourt. I noticed something else too. Set apart from the rest were three police sedans and an ambulance. They stood in a neat and somehow forbidding row, remote from the other vehicles. Those were the transport for the ordinary mortals, the ones who'd only come here for a little fun, a few laughs. These were the harsh reality of the world, the law and disaster.

When I got out the patrol officer was standing watching me.

'Inside,' he commanded.

I led the way in. Two men in the brown uniforms of the County Sheriff's office looked at me with interest.

'Who's this?' barked one.

'This is Preston,' replied my escort.

They both came to life then, staring at me with hard-eyed suspicion.

'O.K., thanks.'

'I'll take him into the sheriff,' offered my man.

'No, it's O.K., we'll handle it. Thanks for bringing him in.'

They wanted me all to themselves. The highway patrol comes under the jurisdiction of the State Police. This was County business. They didn't need anybody else interfering. The patrol man hesitated, shrugged and went away.

'All right you. Wait here,' snapped the red-faced one. He went out through a door off the hall.

I turned to his companion.

'Would you tell me exactly what I'm here for?' I demanded.

'The Sheriff'll deal with you,' he replied curtly. 'You know what's good for you, you'll speak up clear and pretty when he talks to you. That can be a mean man, that Sheriff.'

'Please, I'm shaking all over.'

He grinned. It made his face even more unpleasant.

'Tough,' he observed. 'Sheriff likes tough boys. He'll make mincemeat outa you.'

The other one came back and jerked his head

185

towards the door.

'In here.'

I walked into the room. It was empty.

'Through there.'

Red-face pushed me without gentleness to a door which stood open at the far side of the room. I went through, and found myself in the manager's office, the same Calvin Foyle I'd talked to a few hours before. There were two men standing watching my entrance. I knew the County Sheriff by sight, a beetle-browed squat figure of a man named Kane. The other one was a stranger. At least, the other one standing was a stranger. The man on the floor, twisted in a grotesque pattern of death was Calvin Foyle. Kane's disagreeable voice greeted me.

'So you're Preston, eh?'

'So you're Kane, eh?' I returned.

He flushed a mottled purple.

'I'm Sheriff Kane,' he reminded me. 'And watch your manners when you talk to me.'

'I'm Mr Preston,' I countered. 'And I know it's too late to do anything about your manners.'

'That does it,' he shouted. 'I'm booking you.'

The other one hadn't spoken, but from outward appearances he seemed like a human being. Now he said,

'Hold on, Brad. Let's not fly off the handle.'

His voice was a pleasant baritone sound, and the contrast with Kane's was not to the sheriff's advantage.

'My name is Foster, Milt Foster. I'm with the County Prosecutor's Office,' he said to me. 'We seem to have got off to a bad start. Are you Mark Preston, the private investigator?'

I admitted that I was, and we shook hands. Friendly or not he was still in the same camp as Kane, and I didn't even know whether the war was any of my business. Foster pointed to the body.

'Do you know this man?'

I shook my head.

'I only ever spoke to him once, for about five minutes. That would hardly count as knowing somebody.'

Foster smiled.

'That would depend, wouldn't it? Think of all that can be said in five minutes. You could agree to shoot off a hydrogen bomb in that time.'

'True,' I agreed. 'But we didn't. We didn't even mention the bomb.'

The smile became slightly strained.

'When was this peaceful conversation?'

187

'This afternoon.'

'Ah,' he sounded pleased. 'Exactly what time?'

'I didn't write it down. Must have been somewhere between two and three o'clock.'

He consulted a small leather pocket notebook.

'The bartender says it was around two-twenty. Would you want to argue with that?'

'I never argue with bartenders.'

'Good. Now would you mind telling us what you wanted with Foyle?'

'Yes, I would,' I complained. 'This guy has a business, probably a family. Hundreds of people know him, maybe some of them hate him for all I know. Why should I be rail-roaded in here like an escaped con? I never laid eyes on him except that one time.'

Kane had been restraining himself with difficulty.

'This is a fat waste of time, Mr Foster. Let's get the guy over to the County seat. I'll soon get some better co-operation than this.'

'Sure, Mr Foster, go ahead,' I suggested. 'One more guy beaten to death in that pigpen and you'll all be on the breadline.'

Kane went white, and even the bland Foster seemed taken off his guard momentarily. The County Sheriff's office had a bad record for its treatment of prisoners and even suspects. A few months earlier an old vagrant had died after a brutal beating, and a lot of wires had been pulled to breaking point to keep Kane out of a courtroom. But he wouldn't be so lucky if it happened again.

Foster said distinctly.

'Mr Preston, you will leave me no alternative but to request the sheriff to take you in custody if you persist in this vein. You asked just now why you should be singled out for questioning out of all the people who must have known Foyle. Very well, I will tell you. Do you recognise this?'

He held out a slim white card. I didn't need more than a glance to know what it was.

'Sure. It's one of my cards. I left it with Foyle today in case he ever needed my services. You'll probably find a drawer in his desk with dozens of other people's cards in it.'

'Probably,' nodded Foster. 'But this was the only one we found in the dead man's hand.'

And I hadn't got a quick answer to that one. Foster noted my silence with some satisfaction.

'When the victim was found,' he went on, 'he wasn't quite dead. He said one word several times before he died. That word was Preston. Why do you suppose he would repeat your name that way, and with his dying breath?'

Again I could make no bid.

'I don't know,' I admitted. 'Are you sure of this?'

'We're sure,' gritted Kane. 'And we can make it stand up.'

'I presume you are licensed to carry a gun?' queried Foster.

'Sure. I have a .38 Police Special.'

'Foyle was killed with a .38,' he told me. 'Where is the weapon now?'

'It's right here.'

I pulled it from inside my coat. Kane gasped with alarm and scrabbled frantically for the pouched weapon at his hip. Quickly I handed the .38 to Foster.

'You better have this before that madman kills me.'

Foster had lost some colour himself when I pulled the gun, but he was a quick recoverer. He laughed jerkily.

'I'm sure you have nothing to worry about on that score, eh, Brad?'

If anything, Kane was disappointed.

'If he hadn't of give it to you real quick I'da blown his head off,' he grunted.

It was small comfort to me to know that he meant every word.

'You might care to ask how it came about that Mr Preston walked in here with a gun, considering all the circumstances,' suggested Foster.

'Don't worry,' growled the sheriff. 'Somebody's gonna lose a badge for this.'

Foster nodded, and stood holding my gun on the flat of his palm as though weighing it.

'So you see where we stand, Mr Preston. Today you talked with Foyle. Tonight somebody killed him with a .38 calibre automatic, the same calibre as your own weapon. He muttered your name as he died, and he was holding your business card in his hand. We would like these things explained.'

'You and me both,' I confessed. 'When was the body found?'

'At eight forty-five,' he informed me. 'The dead man was in the habit of taking a meal in his office from 7.45 till 8.45 each evening. The waiter came in for the dishes as usual, and found the manager as you now see him.'

'I see. So if he was still alive, he must have been shot just a few minutes before, huh?'

'No,' he contradicted. 'The medical examiner will naturally need to make a detailed examination, but it seems Foyle did not die immediately. There is medical evidence that he had been shot for some time before he was discovered. He was dying of course, and would

191

never have had the strength, for instance, to get to the door or the telephone. But the doctor says there is every indication the wounds were inflicted between seven forty-five and eight-fifteen. Did I say something amusing?'

'No, I'm sorry.'

I meant it. I don't usually bust a rib when I'm standing next to a corpse. But what had begun to look like a very awkward situation had suddenly blown back into Kane's face.

'I guess you'd like to know where I was between those times this evening?' I offered.

'Yeah,' breathed Kane nastily. 'And make it awful good, won't you. Because anything that can be broken, I'll break.'

'I know that, Kane. I guess I better come clean with you guys.'

'Aha.' The ugly features of the sheriff contorted with evil pleasure. 'There you are, Mr Foster. All that sweet talk, it gets you nowhere with guys like this. You gotta know how to handle these characters who think they're smooth. Come on, smooth boy, something about coming clean, wasn't it?'

'It was.'

I deliberately let him build himself up. I can usually summon up a little respect for a police officer, even the toughest kind. But a thing like Kane is not only an insult to the badge, he's

192

an affront to humanity in general. For him there was only loathing.

'Between seven forty-five and eight fifteen, give or take a minute or two, I was downtown talking to a man,' I announced.

Kane's brow darkened.

'Thought you was coming clean?' he snarled.

'This is as clean as I can get,' I assured him.

'Who was this upright citizen who makes an alibi? The mayor of the city?'

'Not quite. Captain of Detectives, Homicide Squad, Monkton City P.D.,' I said flatly.

'Rourke?' he breathed in disbelief.

'That's the name,' I replied delightedly. 'Do you know him too?'

Kane was speechless but not Foster.

'This will be checked, of course.'

'Of course. In fact, I demand it,' I told him. 'I want this moron off my back.'

Without speaking, Foster picked up the telephone and dialled. Then he spoke, in a calm low voice. He asked one or two questions, politely then put the receiver down.

'It's true.'

'I don't believe it.'

Kane rushed at me, grabbed me by the lapels. If he'd done it a few moments sooner, I wouldn't have been certain what to do. Now

I was certain. I let him have a short left and right to the middle, and not too high up. He gave a great whooshing noise and fell away from me. I waited to see if there would be some more.

'That's all, sheriff,' snapped Foster.

The crisp words seemed to penetrate the heavy fog of rage. Kane stood swaying and breathing painfully. Foster came and stood beween us.

'I'll tell you this, Preston,' and his voice was unfriendly. 'You haven't said a damned word to make anybody love you since you came in here. But I have to admit you couldn't have killed Foyle. I'll want to see you again, perhaps tomorrow, but right now I advise you to get out of here.'

It was a pity, I thought. This was a man I could have got along with if he kept better company.

'Well,' he demanded. 'Are you going?'

I pointed.

'You're holding my property.'

With an impatient snort he held out the automatic and I stuck it back inside my coat.

'When you want me,' I told him, 'You'll know where I am. It's on the card.'

I went out without another glance at Kane. Not without a last look at what had once been

Calvin Foyle. In my own mind I had little doubt that he'd had something to tell me. Something somebody else didn't want me to hear. Something big enough for the somebody to kill Foyle to prevent my finding it out. Outside, the two deputies looked at me in some surprise.

'Disappointed, huh?' I greeted them. 'Never mind, fellers. Even if you don't grab a suspect for the killing tonight, there's always an old vagrant around somewhere.'

They made growling noises, and I made good time through the door and out.

CHAPTER 14

Ten minutes later the Chev slid out of the hugging secrecy of the tree-lined private road and purred to a halt outside the Augustin house. The moon was only half-grown, and a medium wind had sprung up, giving the tall trees plenty of action. In the half-light, and with the anonymous rustlings and whisperings of the wind, the house would have made a good opening shot for one of those old-style horror movies. All that was lacking was the lightning and the banging of a loose shutter. A loose shutter banged, and I turned nervously as I climbed up to the front door. There was no sign of Dracula.

The brass tiger's head looked at me sourly as I raised it and thumped it hard against the heavy door. After a moment or two a chink of light showed at the side of the door as hall-lights were switched on. A woman stood inspecting me with no more than moderate interest. She was sufficiently like Charles Augustin for me to know I was looking at his sister, Mrs Chappel. Although the resemblance was striking her good looks had an extra something that was missing from Charles' features, and the extra something was strength.

'Yes?' she enquired politely.

'I'd like to see Mr Augustin or Mrs Augustin Senior, please. My name is Preston.'

She made no move to let me in.

'What about, Mr Preston?' she asked coolly.

'I think that's something I should discuss with them, don't you?' I countered.

She smiled, very faintly.

'What you think is a matter of no interest to me, Mr Preston. State your business.'

This one could annoy me if she really put her mind to it.

'Mrs—or Miss—' I paused significantly.

'Mrs Chappel,' she supplied.

'Mrs Chappel,' I acknowledged. 'I am calling on Mr Augustin in his own home. I don't see why I should discuss my business with you.'

'You are mistaken, Mr Preston. Evidently you have made a genuine mistake, and that is understandable. This is not Mr Augustin's home. If he has one, which I doubt, it is certainly not here. This is my house, and I shall decide whom I permit to enter. At the moment I am not disposed to have you inside. Now, shall we begin again?'

To say I was non-plussed would have been an under-statement. I was still figuring how to get over that one when a voice called.

'What the devil's going on? That you, Preston?'

Charles Augustin appeared in the hall behind his sister.

'This man seems to be someone you know, Charles, and that in itself seems adequate reason for me to keep him outside.'

Her voice was without inflection but somehow chilling as she spoke to him.

Augustin flushed quickly.

'You're certainly playing your hand for all it's worth, aren't you, Martha? What do you want, Preston?'

197

'I wanted to have a word with you about what happened here today. I also wanted to see Mrs Augustin.'

'Why?' he demanded.

I sighed.

'Do you mean why do I want to talk about your father's death, or why do I want to see your stepmother?'

'Both,' he snapped nastily. 'Especially Avis. What business can you have with her?'

'That's something I'll discuss with her,' I informed him.

'Suit yourself,' he shrugged. 'You were quite right, Martha. Toss this guy out.'

Instead of closing the door, Martha Chappel looked at me thoughtfully.

'I'm getting more used to him. Who are you, Mr Preston? It's evident you're not an intimate of my brother's.'

'I'm a private investigator,' I replied. 'I was here when your father's body was discovered.'

'Oh, yes, that was the name, Preston,' she said half to herself. 'You must forgive my not recalling it, but this has been rather an upsetting day. I think you may come in.'

'Thank you.'

I stepped inside. Augustin looked at me stonily.

'Look, Martha, this man is nothing but a parasite, one of those people who digs up slime for divorce cases. We don't want him here.'

'This way, Mr Preston.'

She ignored him, and led me into a spacious but comfortable room off the hall. Augustin tagged along, like some yapping puppy.

'He's only here to peddle some of his filth, to sell his silence, I tell you.'

Martha Chappel paid him no attention whatever. She sat down arranging her skirt carefully around slim brown legs.

'Please sit down, Mr Preston. It isn't every day I get to meet someone even my brother considers a parasite. You must be unusually loathsome.'

She said it with a merry lilt to her voice that robbed the words of any offence. I perched in a deep armchair and felt myself sink into the luxurious depths. It was not a chair for sitting in, but strictly for falling asleep.

Augustin hovered around, glaring at each of us in turn. I followed his sister's cue and ignored him.

'You seem to have our undivided attention,' she said next. 'Now, why are you here?'

'Firstly, I wanted to tell your brother I didn't think much of that stunt he pulled on me this morning.'

'Stunt?'

She raised an eyebrow. I told her about the removal of the suicide gun from her father's hand.

'Yes, I knew about that,' she agreed.

'It wasn't any of your business,' interjected Charles.

'But you're wrong. It became my business, just by the mere fact of my being here. For anyone in my line, it can be very serious if the police suspect you of meddling with important evidence in a major crime.'

'That's tough,' he sneered. 'That's too bad. I hope you lose your licence.'

'What I am going to lose is my temper, if you don't start being more polite,' I promised him. 'Think yourself lucky, Mrs Chappel is here. One reason I came was to punch you on the nose.'

She chuckled.

'Don't mind me, Mr Preston. Consider the place at your disposal.'

'Oh, you'd like that, wouldn't you?' shouted Charles. 'To have me beaten up by this legalised gangster. God, haven't you caused enough viciousness for one day?'

'It's getting late, Charles,' she reminded him. 'Don't forget you still have to find somewhere to spend the night.'

'Don't worry, I'm going. I wouldn't take any charity from you.'

'There isn't going to be any. I thought I'd made that quite clear,' she stated coldly. 'Mr Preston, you haven't yet said why you want to see Avis Augustin.'

The tone in which she referred to Avis told me there was no love lost in that direction either. At a quick guess, I'd have said Martha knew all about her brother and her stepmother. Carefully I said,

'It isn't so much that I want to talk to her, Mrs Chappel. It's more that I would like to see her, know that she's all right.'

Charles caught his breath. His sister said,

'I don't quite understand. Why shouldn't she be all right?'

'I don't know. I can't give you a sound reason. In this business you learn to develop an instinct for trouble before it happens. I have one of these feelings about Mrs Augustin. Call it a hunch. I shall look ridiculous when she walks in here in a minute, looking hale and hearty. I don't mind looking ridiculous at times like that, in fact I prefer it. It's one of those times it'll be a pleasure to be wrong.'

She looked at me curiously.

'These hunches of yours, are they supposed to be infallible?'

'No,' I said thankfully. 'I'm wrong as often as I'm right.'

'Pah,' sneered Charles. 'Now he's a witch doctor. Look, Preston, why don't you get to the part where you ask about the money?'

'What money?' I asked evenly.

'The money you want for not spilling your filth to the yellow sheets, that's what money. You don't fool me with any of this other nonsense. It's blackmail you guys thrive on, and that's what you're here for.'

I clenched my fists, but stayed where I was.

'Keep talking, Charles,' encouraged his sister. 'I think you're liable to collect that punch on the nose any second now.'

'You think so?' he cried wildly. 'Well, ask him to deny it. Get him to say that's not why he's here.'

'That's not why I'm here,' I said grimly. 'Excuse me, Mrs Chappel.'

I came upright very fast. Charles threw up his hands quickly, but I was in no mood for a Golden Gloves contest. I hit him hard in the middle, again, and then snapped back his head with a wild right. He keeled over backwards and crashed to the floor.

'I'm sorry about that,' I apologised.

Martha's eyes were shining.

'You needn't be,' she said glowingly. 'Somebody ought to have done that to him years ago. He might have been a different man. I have been wishing all day I was a man so that I could do it myself. Let me see your hand.'

I held it out and she looked at the split skin over the knuckle.

'That will hurt tomorrow. Shall I put something on it?'

'No, thanks.'

'A drink, at least,' she insisted. 'Let me get you a large something. Scotch and—?'

'—nothing. Just as it comes.'

She went over to a cupboard and lifted out a square bottle. Tipping out a generous helping, she brought me the glass.

'Thank you. Aren't you having something?'

She shook her head.

'I don't drink a great deal. Besides I got my lift just now, when you did that.'

She gestured towards the crumpled figure of her brother.

'There doesn't seem to be any love lost between you, if you don't mind my saying so.'

'Say on,' she invited. 'My brother is about as worthless a specimen as you could dredge up. Having a lot of money is not necessarily the best background a man can grow up with, Mr Preston. If the man is weak or vain or greedy, he can be a blot on the community.

203

Charles is such a blot, always has been. I'm convinced he drove my father to—to what happened today.'

There was a catch in her throat, quickly controlled.

'My dear brother and the little gutter tramp my father was pleased to bring here as my stepmother. Not a very nice combination for an old man to face up to.'

I tried hard to look non-committal.

'Please don't be embarrassed,' she went on. 'I know exactly what you saw here this morning. It wasn't the first time. Charles wasn't even the first man, there were many others. What makes a man like my father, a hardheaded and widely respected business figure, go and marry a creature like Avis?'

'It's one of the mysteries of the twentieth century,' I consoled. 'And of most other centuries, according to the history books.'

'I suppose so,' she conceded. 'Yes, I'm sure you're right. Why should you think anything bad might happen to her? I mean we all know what she is, but you must know something about her life that I don't. Something which would connect with this intuition of yours.'

I set my glass down on the floor between my feet.

'There are some very odd things going on,

Mrs Chappel.'

I told her about Jeff Hawkins and how normal procedure had brought me to her father. Then I mentioned my visit to the Beano Club that afternoon, and the vague connection with her father's stolen car.

'I went to the Beano Club again tonight,' I concluded. 'Came straight here from there. The man I spoke to, the manager, had just been murdered.'

She gasped with horror.

'But that's terrible. There can't be any connection of course—'

'The connection is unshakeable,' I interrupted. 'The manager—his name was Foyle—was holding my business card in his hand when they found him. He mentioned my name as he died.'

'Good Lord.'

She got up suddenly and paced around, thinking. Then, just as abruptly, she came and sat down again.

'This is quite a shock, I need hardly tell you. People like that. Murder. And—'

She waved a hand around to embrace the house, and everything it stood for. Respectability, position, money.

'Let's hope the connection with your family is no more than a remote coincidence, Mrs

Chappel,' I said gently.

She nodded.

'Yes, yes of course. I'm sure you must be right. There will be some perfectly rational explanation. These things, they have no place here.'

These things have a place everywhere, lady. I decided it was time for me to go.

'I mustn't take up any more of your time.'

I emptied the last of the drink and got up to leave. Augustin stirred suddenly and sat upright, cradling his jaw in his hand. He looked at me balefully, but said nothing. Martha walked with me to the hall.

'If Avis Augustin comes here, or lets you know where she is, would you mind having someone call me?' I requested. 'I'll feel a lot easier.'

'I'll call you myself,' she promised. 'And Mr Preston.'

'H'm?'

I turned in the doorway. She held out a hand.

'Good luck.'

'Thank you.'

As I started the motor I looked up at the house. Martha Chappel was still framed in the doorway. She looked very small against the vast bulk of the house, a slender figure to be carrying the weight of all the responsibility left by her father. That was a burden she'd have to carry alone, unless you counted Charles. And it didn't seem to me that you could.

I yawned prodigiously as I rolled between the tall trees. It was almost midnight and I wanted sleep. But there were still a couple of things to be done before I was going to get any. Ahead, in the distance, the neon pattern of Monkton City sparkled like a man-made jewel against the black horizon. The trouble with jewels is, they sometimes have flaws. And the flaws were my business.

CHAPTER 15

Twenty minutes later I was leaning on the buzzer at No. 1616 Alohah Apartments. I sensed, rather than heard, that someone was standing on the other side of the door.

'Who's there?' demanded a man's voice suspiciously.

That would be Jack Wells, Heather's boy friend. I was glad he was taking sensible precautions.

'It's me, Preston,' I told the door.

'Oh,' he sounded relieved. 'Just a moment.'

A bolt rattled inside. The door opened and I stepped inside. Something hard crunched at the side of my head and I fell to my knees as the blinding pain exploded in my skull. Hands prodded at me and I felt the .38 sliding out from my coat. Gradually the red fog grew thinner and I could see something swaying about in front of me. I grabbed it, and it was a chairleg. I climbed up the front of the chair and stood leaning heavily against it. Somebody laughed.

'Stop that,' cut in a sharp voice. 'I can't tolerate mockery of those in pain. How are you feeling, Preston?'

I turned a bleary eye towards the voice and saw Kingsland Powell's anxious face watching me. He smiled in a friendly way that would have been more convincing if he hadn't been pointing a heavy revolver at me. I let go of the chair and half-turned. My knees caved in and a quick grab at the chair helped me defeat gravity.

By the door there was a goon I'd never laid eyes on before. In his hand was a leather sap, and he swung it meaningly to let me know that was what hit me. Heather, the maid, sat with her arms round a dark-skinned man who had to be Wells. He seemed to be unconscious. At the far end of the room, smoking furiously and looking very bad-tempered, was Julie

Van Dorn. So naturally, the brightest opening remark I could offer was,

'I thought you didn't smoke?'

She glared at me, but didn't answer.

Powell chuckled appreciatively.

'I declare, Preston, you really are an extremely self-possessed fellow. Yes, I must say, you have a certain panache.'

I swayed round towards him and tried to look tough.

'I have a certain lump on the side of my head that somebody's going to pay for,' I croaked.

He shook his head and tutted.

'But that unfortunate memory doesn't improve at all. Once again, you have forgotten this.'

He reminded me about the gun.

'So kill somebody,' I suggested. 'Me, I'm going to have a drink.'

I performed a rather graceless parade round the room until I located Julie.

'Is there a drink in the house lady?' I begged.

She snorted and went out of my view. Seconds later a cold glass was stuck in my fist.

'I hope it chokes you,' she said.

I tipped up the glass, and it held brandy. The warmth of it spread through me. I was feeling better all the time, but didn't want the fact to register with Powell.

'All right, Preston, I think that's all the convalescence I can spare you,' he clipped suddenly. 'And now, we'll have no more delays. I want your end of our bargain, and I want it now.'

'You got the money?' I stalled.

'The money is something we'll discuss after I've checked the goods,' he demurred. 'So?'

I sat down with a thump and put my head in my hands.

'I'm waiting, Preston.'

'So you are, Powell, so you are. You're in a spot, aren't you?'

He smiled mirthlessly.

'I really don't see how I can agree with that. I have the gun. My associate over there has another. You have one unconscious man and two women to help you. I would say that any disadvantage lies with you.'

'You would?' I sneered. 'But I have the stuff, and I'm going to keep it. You might get rough, you might even get downright nasty. But you're not going to butcher four people, just like that. You're a business man, and besides, it's not St Valentine's Day.'

Julie suddenly came to life.

'I was a fool to listen to you, Preston. Well, I won't make the same mistake twice. If anything happens here, I'm going to hold you personally responsible. You got three innocent people involved in this filth and whatever happens to any of them is something you'll answer for. Come on, get up.'

She leaned down, grabbed my lapels and heaved. In the effort, her head came down beside mine, and her face was out of Powell's sight.

'Fight back,' she whispered quickly.

I came reluctantly to my feet.

'Look, stop it will you?' I protested feebly.

Her hand came round with stinging force, and I felt it hard on my face. I backed away.

'Cut it out, or I'll slap you, so help me,' I warned.

'Oh, sure. Big hero,' she jeered. 'No good at fighting the men, but a big hand at beating up women.'

She hit me again, and again. I backed off.

'I'm warning you—' I began.

'Pig' she shouted.

In abandoned fury she flung herself at me, her arms going like pistons. I threw up my hands defensively and moved back as fast as I could. We were only a couple of feet from Powell, who was watching with amusement. To ward off the flurry of blows to my face I crossed my hands in front of it. Julie stood back and began to swing a wild wide right. Just as it was about to land she brought both feet up off the floor and kicked straight ahead of her. In the way was Kingsland Powell, and it all happened too fast for him even to register surprise. The spiked heels bit into his hand and the gun clattered to the floor. I was already down and groping for it before the goon at the door realised the danger.

'Hey,' he shouted suddenly, diving into his pocket.

I didn't wait to find out whether it was a cigarette case in there. Turning on my knees I put a bullet in his shoulder, and he shouted again, and clapped his hand over the hole.

'Heather, get his gun,' I ordered. 'And be careful.'

Powell was nursing at his bloody hand and was pale with rage. Julie lay on the floor, all the wind knocked out of her. As she kicked Powell she had fallen horizontally to the floor and this is not the best way to fall.

'You all right?' I asked.

She nodded, then realised her skirt had kicked up all around her middle. Blushing quickly, she wriggled it down.

'A most resourceful young woman. I must congratulate you, Preston,' Powell remarked quietly. 'You seem to have reversed the position here, so there is no point in our remaining.

If you'll excuse us, Mrs Van Dorn, we'll be running along.'

He began to walk towards his wounded companion. Julie got up and looked at me with wide eyes.

'Is this guy for real?' she demanded.

I grinned.

'He takes some getting used to,' I explained. 'Hold it, Powell. Nobody's going anywhere.'

He turned, and managed to look surprised.

'I'm afraid I don't quite follow. I came here to do business. As I understand it, you are not interested. Since you appear to have the advantage in—a—other ways, we seem to have reached a stalemate.'

'No,' I contradicted. 'What we seem to have reached is the end of the line for you and buddy-boy there, that's all. Come back here and sit down. No, Heather.'

I shouted suddenly. Heather had the gun she'd taken from the other man's pocket and was swinging it at Powell's head. He ducked and it passed harmlessly through the air. She said furiously.

'That's what they did to poor Jack. He never had a chance either.'

'You'd do more good for Jack if you got a cold compress for that head, and tried to bring

213

him round,' I grunted.

I took the gun away from her and slipped it in my pocket. It was my own .38 anyway. To Julie I said,

'You ever shoot one of these things?'

'I'm an expert,' she replied. 'Shooting was my husband's hobby.'

'O.K.'

I gave her the revolver and told Powell to sit.

'If he tries to get out of that chair, use this. Don't point it at his head. Aim for his middle. You can't miss and you'll do more damage.'

She nodded grimly and from the look on her face I'd have sat quietly if I'd been Powell. He evidently agreed with me. I went to the other man, who was leaning painfully by the door, cursing slowly and steadily.

'Cut that out,' I told him. 'Let's have a look at the scratch.'

He didn't want to take his hand from the wound, so I pulled it clear, and I wasn't in the mood to be gentle.

'Take it easy,' he protested.

'You're lucky I don't beat on it with your sap,' I told him. 'Who are you and where do you figure?'

He stared at me dumbly. Bending down, I retrieved the leather sap from the carpet where he'd dropped it.

'I'm waiting,' I reminded him.

'Drop dead,' he invited.

I swung the sap against the door. It made a solid dull thud.

'H'm,' I observed conversationally. 'Heavy. Now we'll try the shoulder.'

I swung it again lightly, and tapped at the damaged shoulder a few inches away from the bullet-hole. He yelped as much in fear as from real pain, but still said nothing.

'That was just testing for range,' I warned him. 'Next one will be on the target.'

He clenched his teeth, and glared his hate. I shrugged and raised my arm. This time I brought it down much harder. Before I made contact he ducked suddenly.

'You ain't human,' he said wonderingly. 'The name is Heffer. Art Heffer.'

'Better. And what is all this to you?'

'Nothin', honest. I'm working for him, for the little guy. He says it's good money and a little exercise. I never figured on nobody like you.'

'Do you know what it's all about, this little argument?'

He shook his head vigorously.

'That's not my business. I get paid to do as I'm told.'

I believed him.

215

'How much did he promise?'

'Fifty. I musta bin crazy. Ouch.'

Another twinge of pain from the shoulder forced a small cry from him. I went to where Powell was sitting.

'You owe the man fifty dollars.'

'Really, Preston, I fail to see that any arrangement I may have had with Mr Heffer is any of your concern.'

'Fifty,' I repeated, holding out a hand.

He grimaced, pulled out some bills. With measured reluctance he peeled off two twenties and a ten.

'Here,' he said grudgingly.

'Thanks.'

I reached across and tweaked another twenty from the roll.

'For bandages,' I explained.

Heffer watched this performance open-mouthed. I went back to him and stuffed the bills in his top pocket.

'You've been paid, plus a little something for the damage. You got any complaints?'

'I knew it before,' he muttered. 'You're plain nuts.'

'Can you get that shoulder fixed without dragging in a lot of uniforms?'

He nodded.

'Sure.'

'Then beat it.'

'Huh?'

'I said "beat it," ' I repeated.

I opened the door, and waited. He took a half-step, halted.

'You mean it?'

'I mean it. If you get picked up, do your own explaining. Just leave this out.'

He made his painful way through the door and was gone. Powell laughed.

'Against my better judgment, Preston, I'm compelled to admit that crossing your path has been a diverting experience. Yes, I think I may say that. Diverting.'

'Did you kill Calvin Foyle tonight?' I demanded.

He looked puzzled.

'Who is Mr Foyle exactly? And no, I did not kill him.'

'He's the manager of a place called the Beano Club. Or he was, until a few hours ago. Somebody put some lead in him.'

'Ah, the Beano Club,' he nodded as if understanding. 'Yes, I think I can follow that. And I may even be able to suggest the name of the person who—ah—eliminated Mr Foyle.'

'Really? Like who?'

'Your employer, Nielson. He may well have had good reason for wanting Mr Foyle out of the way. Please, I can see you are about to question me and I should like to spare you the trouble. I haven't the least idea what those reasons might be. But I could well believe they exist.'

The maddening thing about Powell was that he always seemed perfectly relaxed. Now he leaned back and crossed his knees, for all the world like a favoured guest at a house-party.

'You still want to trade?' I demanded.

'Of course,' he assured me. 'That was the purpose of my little visit.'

'Get up.' I ordered.

'I'm quite comfortable here, thank you.'

'Get up,' I repeated.

To give emphasis to the words I grabbed him under the arm and heaved. He couldn't have weighed more than one twenty.

'Hold your hands up.'

Sighing his disapproval he did as I asked. I ran my hands over him from behind. There was something tucked inside his pants at the rear. I pulled it out and found a slim plastic envelope. Inside were ten pieces of paper. Each one was marked 'One thousand dollars'.

'Go ahead,' invited Julie. 'Attack him.'

She was talking to Powell, who had evidently considered it. Now he looked quickly at her, and at the cold black ring of metal pointing at his stomach.

'You're a very unorthodox fellow, Preston,' he said coldly. 'I must confess I'm disappointed. I had expected a certain—what shall I say? not honour, exactly—code of conduct. Yes, that is precisely the phrase I was seeking. I did not expect, sir, this kind of tactic from such as yourself. I am assuming you do not propose to fill your end of the transaction.'

'Can't do it,' I told him. 'You can sit down again, now.'

He bowed slightly and dropped back into the chair.

'I urge you to make the most of this brief, and quite tawdry triumph,' he said, and now the evil was back in his tone. 'You completely realise, I trust, that I shall kill you for this?'

Heather gasped with sudden horror. I'd almost forgotten she was there.

'How's Jack, honey?' I queried.

'I think he'll be all right,' she replied over her shoulder. 'He's starting to come round.'

'Good. Julie, can we go in another room? I want to talk to this guy, and he won't say too much in front of all these people.'

'Surely,' she nodded. 'Let's go in the bedroom.'

'A waste of time, dear lady. I have no intention

of talking to your friend, in there or anywhere else,' Powell informed her.

'We'll see. Move.'

We all trooped into the bedroom and I shut the door. Powell looked around and clucked with appreciation.

'I hardly expected a woman with your taste in friends to have such an appreciation for lovely things.'

'Sit on the bed,' I said.

He sat carefully, running appraising fingers over the silk spread.

'Powell, I ought to give you to the law, but instead I'm giving you a chance to walk out of here,' I began.

'Very interesting. Pray continue,' he begged.

'In addition, I am willing to give you back the money. All of it.'

This made a much bigger impression.

'I declare, Mr Preston, you're a man of many surprises. And now, may I know exactly what you expect in return for such magnanimity?'

Julie chuckled richly.

'I don't know where you found this character, Preston, but he'd be a natural in Hollywood.'

'In Hollywood the guns have blanks,' I pointed out. 'This comedian is the genuine article. But you're right, Powell. I want something in return. And the something is information.'

He cleared his throat.

'Naturally. I hope you will accept it when I tell you I am by nature an extremely close-mouthed man. However I am compelled to admit to you that the money places me at some disadvantage. You see, it is not mine. I have been entrusted with it by those powerful business interests about whom I spoke to you earlier. I fear they may take it unkindly if they learn that I have failed. In brief, sir, what do you wish to know?'

'First, did you ever hear of a young man named Jeffrey Hawkins?'

He puckered his finely modelled brows.

'No. One meets many people of course, but I think not.'

'He died in a car smash a few months back,' I prompted.

'One is always distressed to hear of a young life being ended,' he commented. 'But the name is still not familiar.'

The man was so full of humbug, I didn't know whether to believe him or not.

'All right. Second, who's Nielson?'

He looked up in surprise.

'Nielson? Are we playing games, Mr Preston? Nielson, I am quite positive, is known to you. Indeed, you have led me to believe he is your principal in this matter.'

'Yes,' I agreed, 'I did. It seemed to be a good way of keeping myself in this caper, so I let you think it. I never heard of Nielson until you mentioned him. Now I find him an interesting man. Who is he?'

Powell shook with silent laughter, and passed a hand over his face. He finished his laugh before replying.

'Mr Preston, I have suddenly realised something. I can only plead unusually trying circumstances as an excuse for not realising this sooner. Mr Preston, I mean no offence when I say it, but I fear you are a fraud, sir. Yes, a fraud. It dawns on me suddenly, and rather late in the game, that you are blundering in the dark. Why, do you know what I am now thinking? I will tell you. I believe you know nothing about this business whatever. Without wishing to be impolite, I think you are an impostor.'

He looked at me for confirmation. I grinned and inclined my head.

'If you'd thought of it earlier,' I admitted. 'I'd still be out there in the dark. But now I'm in here. I have the money, and the gun. I have you, my dear friend. And whether we like it or not, I'm in it now. And I want answers.

Who is Nielson?'

He held up a hand.

'Permit me a moment to consider my position.'

We all sat around while Powell considered his position. His position was that he was ten thousand dollars in the red, and before he got it back, he'd have to give out some information. I knew he'd tell me as little as he could get away with, but anything was better than the present fog.

'I take it that the position is unchanged in other respects?' he asked, finally. 'To come to the point, sir, will there be any policemen involved?'

'I guarantee nothing,' I told him. 'If anybody was the cause of Jeff Hawkins' death, they are going to pay for it. That could mean police.'

It seemed to satisfy him.

'I accept that,' he nodded. 'Because this young man's death was in no way the concern of myself or my superiors. Yes, I think that will be satisfactory. You asked who Nielson is.'

I tried not to seem impatient. Julie watched us with fascination, but retained a firm grip on the gun.

'Nielson,' and Powell's voice took an edge of menace each time he spoke the name, 'Nielson

223

was a man I trusted. In this precarious world, one tends to trust fewer and fewer people, Mr Preston. But I had faith in Nielson, and he betrayed me.'

His voice trailed away and he became preoccupied with thoughts of Nielson, and it wasn't hard to guess he was dreaming of their next meeting.

'My superiors in another part of the world arranged for a certain package to be brought to this country. The contents were extremely valuable and, unfortunately, readily negotiable anywhere in this great country. It was not the first time such a transaction had taken place. Indeed, it was a regular procedure. The package was delivered to Nielson as usual. His role in the affair was that of a wholesale dealer, if you are familiar with the expression. He would take delivery of the goods, dispose of them, and at an appointed time produce the sum of money which had been agreed. He had done this several times to complete satisfaction of all concerned. On this last occasion, he took the goods but failed to pay. This has been a serious inconvenience to my employers. My trip here is for the purpose of recovering either the merchandise or the money.'

'And killing Nielson,' I commented.

He hunched his shoulders meaningly.

'In a big business, Mr Preston, fair dealing is essential. If Nielson were to be allowed to act in this manner with impunity it would be noted by a number of people who might be similarly tempted.'

'And this stuff is worth ten thousand dollars?'

I pointed to the money.

'Dear me, no. That is spending money, sir. Oil to grease the wheels which will restore the situation. The package is worth at the minimum one hundred and fifty thousand dollars.'

Now I could see what he meant by big business.

'Tell me, do you know whether Nielson was ever paid for the shipment? In other words, are you positive about whether it's the money or the actual goods he's holding?'

'Both. Nielson made the mistake so many have made when finding themselves in a similar position. There is always a brief period, perhaps of only a few minutes, when the money and the goods will be in the same room. This is a situation fraught with possible dangers. It sometimes happens that one of the parties concerned decides to walk off with everything. On this occasion, it was Nielson who made such a decision.'

'So he collected a hundred and fifty grand, and kept the stuff?'

'I regret to say that is correct.'

I whistled.

'Quite a haul. But you're wasting your time, surely? He must be long gone from this town, with a stake like that.'

'True, but he has a mother here, an elderly lady in poor health. He has always been devoted to her. Sooner or later he will get in touch with her, and then I shall have him. My activities in the meantime are devoted to attempting to shorten the waiting period. I must say I really thought I had something when you arrived on the scene, but alas, you are of no value.'

'Who are the people Nielson robbed of the money?' I queried.

Powell smiled, a wide disarming smile.

'I'm afraid there are some things one must keep confidential.'

'All right, tell me this. Was it the Beano Club where the swap was supposed to take place?'

He pondered.

'Well, I imagine there can be little harm in your knowing that. Yes, I believe that was the case. And now, if you're quite satisfied, I must say goodnight.'

Julie came quickly.

'Stay where you are,' she ordered. Then to me, 'You can't just let him walk out like this. Why don't you hand him over to the police?'

I shook my head.

'On what charge? A little breaking in to your apartment, some assault. A smart attorney will have him out and around again in less than a year. Then he might decide to do something about me, or you for that matter. I don't want to spend my whole life looking over my shoulder.'

'But he's going to commit a murder,' she protested.

'That's what he tells us,' I admitted. 'But he hasn't found the guy yet. And there's no law against wanting to murder somebody. If there was half the population would be behind bars.'

Powell listened with grave attention.

'Evidently the young lady is quite unused to this type of situation. I assure you, Mrs Van Dorn, that Mr Preston is giving sound advice.'

'Don't speak to me, you make me sick,' she retorted.

I gave him the money.

'Here. You better beat it before the lady changes my mind.'

227

He got up and pointed at the gun she was holding.

'That is my property, you recall.'

I took it from her and emptied out the shells.

'Not that I don't trust you.'

'I would have done precisely the same,' he assured me. 'Well, I'll get along. I may say, Mr Preston, that I find it a relief we are not in opposite camps. I should have been sorry indeed to see you come to any harm.'

As we walked out to the door, Heather watched in astonishment. He bowed quickly to her, and was gone. Julie Van Dorn said,

'I hope you know what you're doing. How will you feel if that evil little man really kills this Nielson?'

'Terrible,' I assured her. 'But there wasn't anything I could have done that would prevent it, was there?'

'I suppose not,' she conceded grudgingly. 'What happens now?'

'Now, you are out of it, lady,' I replied. 'And I want to thank you for what you've done. Sorry about Jack here getting that clunk on the head.'

She made a little moue of disappointment.

'Perhaps Powell isn't really satisfied. He may still think I've got that package in the apartment somewhere.'

I grinned and wagged my head from side to side.

'No, ma'am. He's satisfied all right. You won't be seeing him again.'

'I see. Was I any help at all? I didn't seem to do much.'

'You did more than most people would have. You stuck out your pretty neck, and I'm grateful. It was more help than you reaise.'

'Will I see you any more?'

She sounded as if the idea wasn't repugnant.

'When this is over I'll come and tell you all about it, if you'd like,' I offered.

'I'd like.'

I wished Heather and her boy-friend were miles away, instead of sitting there pretending not to hear.

'I'll call you,' I promised.

Outside, a chill breeze reminded me it was one in the morning. As I opened the door of the Chev I shivered.

Frank Hawkins said.

'Thought you were going to spend the night in there.'

He sat hunched in the passenger seat. I climbed in beside him and closed the door.

'If it isn't my employer,' I said nastily. 'I didn't expect to see you again. And why does everybody in town think I'm a bus company tonight?'

'I don't get it, but it doesn't matter. How've you been doing?'

'I found out a few things,' I admitted. 'But not much that you couldn't have told me before I started.'

'Huh? How's that again?'

'Tell me one thing. Was your brother mixed up in all this, or are you the only crook in the family?'

CHAPTER 16

He made no reply as I rolled out into the thinning traffic, but stared moodily out at the neon streets.

'What is that supposed to mean?' he erupted suddenly.

'It was plain enough. Some stuff has been smuggled in here on a regular route from the Orient. You're the guy who's been bringing it in.'

'I'm not paying you for a character analysis. Your end is to find out what happened to Jeff. Nothing more.'

I swerved to dodge a late-night driver who thought he could drink as well.

'You're wrong, Hawkins. Everything to do with Jeff touches the other thing I just mentioned. It doesn't take a very smart man to work it out. Your kid brother was in this mess up to his eyes.'

He swivelled quickly towards me.

'You're a liar,' he barked. 'If you weren't driving this thing I'd punch you right in the nose.'

I drove on without speaking. After a moment or two he swung back and resumed his hunchback imitation.

'Ah, what am I getting sore about? Anybody would think what you're thinking, I guess. Maybe I ought to put you straight.'

'It might be of some help,' I agreed. 'And help I could use.'

'Tell me what you've found out, I'll fill in some holes.'

I told him most of what had happened since he first came to see me. He grunted a few times to show he was still awake.

'You've been busy,' he acknowledged, when I finished. 'And what's your answer?'

'I don't know yet. Not definitely. I make you the guy who brought in the stuff—what was it by the way?'

'Never mind that. I brought it in. And?'

'And you delivered to Nielson. Nielson took it to the Beano Club to hand it to somebody. Then he changed his mind, took the money and didn't hand over the goods.'

'Okay so far. Where does Jeff come in?'

'Unless he's implicated, I can't put him in at all.'

'He wasn't mixed up in it, I already told you that,' he snapped.

'Then why is he dead?' I asked softly.

'Yeah,' he breathed. 'That's the big one.'

'Tell me about Nielson,' I suggested. 'You think they'll catch up with him?'

'No doubt about it. Those guys are very thorough. May take years, but they'll find him.'

'How can they be sure he's the one they want?'

'Huh?'

'For example, you might be the one. You could have killed Nielson instead of delivering, and then buried him somewhere while everybody ran round looking for him.'

He didn't even sound offended.

'I could've,' he agreed. 'But I didn't. And I had a rough time with certain people back in Hong Kong until they believed me. They really know how to ask questions over there.

If I'd done that, I'd have been glad to tell them, believe me.'

We were approaching Parkside Towers now. As I eased off the motor, I recognised the black sedan parked out front, pushed my foot down and roared past, ducking my head at the same time.

'What's all that for?' queried Hawkins.

'Police car outside,' I explained.

'You didn't do anything, did you?'

'With those boys I'm never sure. Now and then I have to bend a law or two to get results. Trouble is, I can never be sure what they know and what they don't.'

'So you drive around all night?'

'No. I make a telephone call.'

I stopped outside a late bar and went in to the 'phone.

A man said crisply.

'Police Headquarters.'

'The name is Preston. Got it? There's a squad car outside where I live. Any idea why?'

'Preston, you say? Hold on, Mr Preston.'

There was a lot of clicking and scraping. Finally an excited voice bawled in my ear.

'Preston, zattyou?'

It was Vince Brooks.

'It better be. What are those guys doing

lowering the value of the property over at Parkside?'

He didn't get insulted.

'Those officers are for your protection, citizen. And I personally love you.'

'Nauseating. What did I do?'

'Oh, nothing. Nothing at all. That tip on the Elmans, that was a lulu.'

'So you caught two burglars. Congratulations.'

'Burglars nothing,' he contradicted. 'They own the place. I felt kind of silly for a coupla minutes when we first bust in there. They were going to have *me* arrested. But I poked around the place, practically in desperation. And what did I find?'

'A corpse?' I asked hopefully.

'Better. Enough heroin to kill half the town. We had 'em cold. And you gave me that. Go ahead and break a few laws. There isn't a cop in town will bug you, not tonight.'

'So why do I need protecting?' I asked patiently.

Some of the exuberance went out of his voice.

'Oh, yes. Well, that damned warehouse is a mess for lighting. They knew every inch of it, naturally. They started cutting up on a narrow iron stairway and we lost 'em. But it's only temporary. Now they're actually on the run, every officer has them down for a shoot-on-sight.'

'Great. And meantime, they're probably looking for me.'

'I doubt it. They know we'll have you protected. They'll be too busy looking after their own skins to worry about you. But we're not taking any chances, so go home and get protected.'

I stared at the wall, thinking. According to the wall, if I was lonely, there was a lady named Honeylou who'd be glad to remedy the situation.'

'You still there?' Brooks barked suddenly.

'Yes, I'm here. Tell me, was Georgie Elman wearing glasses when you lost him?'

'Glasses?' he exploded indignantly. 'What kind of question is that?'

'It's important, Vince,' I explained patiently. 'Without his eye glasses the man is practically blind.'

'Oh, I didn't realise. Yes, yes he definitely was wearing a pair. And that's a useful piece of information.'

'You're welcome. So long, Vince.'

He started shouting questions down the phone, but I hung up. My clever idea about busting Georgie's glasses had turned out a bust. He must have had a spare pair somewhere handy after all. Back in the car, Hawkins asked,

'You made a call. Now what?'

I told him what Brooks had said. He sat and digested it carefully.

'So if they had all that H, Nielson must have delivered after all.'

'Seems like it. Was it the Elmans he was supposed to contact?'

'Partly. This changes a lot of things. Just drive, will you. I want to think about this.'

I drove around the empty streets, while Hawkins slumped beside me, deep in thought. I lit an Old Favourite and wondered where the Elmans would make for. Remembering the look on Georgie's face a few hours earlier, I hoped he wouldn't decide to come looking for me. If I had any sense in my head I'd head back to Parkside Towers and those comforting policemen with their nice big guns.

Hawkins' voice suddenly grated into my mind.

'I wasn't going to tell you any of this, Preston. But this bit with the Elmans tonight, that changes too many things. You want to hear a story?'

'I love stories,' I told him.

CHAPTER 17

A solitary light burned in a window near the big doors. I made a lot of noise roaring the motor before switching off, and then slamming the door of the car. Hawkins said,

'All right so you're here. No need to wake up the entire neighbourhood.'

'This is the entire neighbourhood,' I informed him. 'The woman is alone in the house. A sudden bang on the door might give her heart failure or something.'

'But you already telephoned,' he objected.

'I did. And I told her she'd be sure it was me, because I'd make enough noise to wake the dead.'

'Oh.'

Together we went up the stairs. As we reached the door it swung quietly open. Martha Chappel stood looking at us, a heavy shotgun in her hands.

'Come in, Mr Preston. What is your friend's name, please?'

'Hawkins, Mrs Chappel,' he supplied. 'Sorry to be bothering you this time of the night.'

She led us inside, to a small but comfortable room.

'At our last meeting, Mr Preston, you impressed me as a man who'd be unlikely to disturb someone in the middle of the night without a very good reason.'

She was very striking in a red velvet housecoat with large black buttons. Beside me, I could sense Hawkins appreciating her.

'Thank you. I think you'll be more than interested in what I have to say. I only hope it won't be too painful.'

'Let's sit down, shall we? As for your information, Mr Preston, I doubt whether it will be more painful than the rest of the day's events. Please go on.'

'Your father did not get on very well with your brother Charles, I believe?'

'That was common knowledge.'

'All right. Your father also cut off all money allowances to Charles some two years ago.'

'This is all very well known, Mr Preston. If you want it expressed in plain words, my father considered Charles a wastrel, a sponger and worse.'

She spoke calmly, and it was evident the relationship between father and son had long been a part of the accepted scheme of things.

'Worse?' I raised my voice, and made it a question. 'Worse in what way?'

'I don't think we need concern ourselves with that,' she began, '—Or need we?'

'Possibly. Mrs Chappel, I'm trying to be as delicate as I can, but the subject doesn't lend itself to tact,' I told her. 'Are you implying that your father suspected Charles of something criminal?'

She fiddled with one of the big buttons.

'Yes,' she admitted, in a low voice. 'But it was a long time ago.'

'Was it something to do with drugs?' I persisted.

She looked at me in surprise.

'How could you possibly know that? Everything was hushed up.'

I denied that by shaking my head. Hawkins snorted.

'Must be nice to have money,' he remarked bitterly.

'Let me handle this, Frank. Remember, Mrs Chappel didn't ask us here.'

He nodded quickly.

'Mrs Chappel,' I resumed. 'The particular incident your father discovered was not an isolated one. There is every reason to think your brother is involved in the distribution of narcotics.'

Tiny wrinkles gathered in the corners of her eyes.

'I see. You wouldn't be here at two in the morning if you hadn't good reason for saying that.

'I'm glad you realise the position.'

I meant it too. An emotional scene in the middle of the night was something I could do without. Apart from the delay it would cause. Then I said,

'I got the impression earlier today that you and Charles had been quarrelling. Could I ask what about? Unless it's a family matter, of course.'

'There are no family matters between Charles and me,' she informed me. 'There was no quarrel, as you put it. Merely the usual discussion one or other of us is always having with Charles. He wanted money.'

'And you refused?'

'Naturally,' she said severely. 'Giving money to Charles is like giving a baby matches to play with. It's a commodity he doesn't understand. In any case I couldn't have helped him, even if I wanted. He was asking for more money than I have, at least until the estate is settled.'

'Ah yes, the estate. I was going to ask about that. Is Charles a beneficiary under the terms of your father's will?'

'I think you're going too far, Mr Preston,' she advised me calmly. 'Is all of this any of your affair?'

I had hoped to avoid hitting her where it would hurt, but it seemed that the time had come.

'Mrs Chappel, I'm sorry to have to tell you this, but I think your father was murdered. That makes it more your affair than mine.'

'Murdered?' she echoed dully. 'Who'd want to kill him? He was a fine man. Why, I don't know anyone who wished him harm.'

She didn't want to believe it. But the tone she used lacked conviction.

Then the sequence of the questions registered and she said angrily,

'You asked whether Charles inherited anything. You think Charles would have killed father? And for profit? You don't know Charles very well if you think that. He's not much to be proud of, but I know he could never do such a thing. The suggestion is contemptible.'

She was working herself to throwing us out, and that I didn't want. Not yet.

'Nobody suggested it but you,' I pointed out gently. 'Your father's death is only one of a series of incidents which all link together. I'm looking for the answer to the whole problem, and I'm asking these questions to that end, not only to trace whoever killed your father.'

'If he was killed,' she retorted. 'The police think otherwise.'

'The police haven't yet the advantage of certain information that I have. When they do, they'll think the same way,' I assured her.

'It's late, and I'm tired,' she said wearily. 'You may be right, I don't know. Anyway you can forget any ridiculous ideas about Charles. He is named in the will. He is to receive two hundred and fifty dollars and any cars belonging to my father at the time of death. Oh, and before you direct your thinking towards Avis Augustin, let me tell you the size of her inheritance.'

'I know it. It's one hundred dollars.'

'I see. Well, you'd hardly call the combined fortune a motive for murder, would you?'

'No, ma'am, I wouldn't,' I agreed. 'This money Charles wanted to borrow, did he tell you what it was for?'

'He told me a tale. Charles always has a tale, full of high drama and low morals. This time he was supposed to be in serious difficulties with some people who might even take his life. I told him I hadn't got that much money, even if I'd been willing to help him.

He made a terrible scene.'

'He could have been telling the truth this time, Mrs Chappel. Was the sum he asked for a hundred and fifty thousand dollars?'

This time the surprise was wide on her face.

'How could you possibly know that?'

I said urgently,

'Because I believe Charles was telling you the truth for once. I also believe he could be in real danger of losing his life. We've got to find him and protect him. Where is he?'

She seemed bewildered by the sudden change in my attitude.

'Why, I don't know. I haven't the faintest idea where he's gone.'

'Do you know where Avis went?'

'No. We're not exactly friendly. There's no reason why she should tell me what she does. Any pretence of a truce between us need no longer be maintained.'

'Do you think they're together?' I asked brutally.

The pain came into her face and was quickly gone.

'Perhaps.'

'Look, Mrs Chappel, murder has already been done. I think it will be done again if we don't find your brother and Avis Augustin. And quickly. I don't think they would dare stay

243

anywhere in town. Is there anywhere else at all they could go?'

She looked at me doubtfully.

'You're quite serious, aren't you? If the situation is really as bad as you say, I suppose they could be at the cottage.'

'Cottage? Where is it?'

'It hasn't been aired in months, and I don't suppose there's any food in the place—'

'Where, lady? Quick,' snapped Hawkins.

'It's just around the lake. A mile, perhaps less.'

'Is there a road?'

'It's all overgrown,' she protested. 'You'd never find the place if you didn't know the way.'

'Then that's settled,' Hawkins growled. 'You'll have to come and show us.'

'At this hour—' she began.

'It's a matter of life and death,' I told her seriously.

She looked at me, then Hawkins. She must have seen something in our faces that told her this was no time for arguments.

'Wait here, I'll get a coat.'

She went out and was back quickly, wrapped in a heavy outdoor coat. As we trooped silently out to the Chev, I noticed she was walking stiffly. She sat next to me to give directions.

We turned off the drive into a narrow rutted lane that was a tangle of bushes and vines. We couldn't make more than ten miles an hour and every hump jolted us up and down savagely. Twice she had to grab the wheel at some suddenly remembered twist in the road. Altogether, it was not an enjoyable ride.

'How far now?' hissed Hawkins suddenly from the rear.

'About another hundred yards,' she replied.

'What do you say we walk the rest, Preston?' he asked.

'Good idea.'

I switched off the motor. Martha Chappel watched in astonishment.

'What are you doing that for?'

'Mrs Chappel,' I explained. 'When I came to your house tonight I made all kinds of noise. I wanted you to know I was there. This place is different. I don't know who's in there or what I'm going to find. Until I know these things I don't want to be announced.'

'Oh.'

She sounded suddenly frightened, and I didn't blame her.

'No need for you to come. You stay here in the car and wait for us. We probably won't be long.'

'No,' she refused. 'I'd be more scared sitting

out here alone. I'm coming with you.'

'Let her come,' Hawkins interrupted. 'You stay behind me, Mrs Chappel, and don't make any noise. If there's any kind of trouble you get out of there fast.'

'Very well.'

We climbed, clicking the doors gently shut. Something slithered noisily into the dark tangle of growth beside us. Martha Chappel shivered and grabbed my arm. I felt as brave as hell.

'Indian file,' I whispered. 'Me first, Hawkins, Mrs Chappel.'

Hawkins grunted his assent and I set off the way the car was pointing. A full moon would have been a help, but may have proved a handicap when we got to the cottage. I plodded slowly forward, arms stretched out ahead. I stumbled several times, banged my hands against a lot of tree trunks that would have done my head no good at all. Thin bramble-covered arms tore at my face, but gradually we made ground. I was beginning to think Martha's idea of a hundred yards should have been a hundred miles when suddenly I arrived at the edge of a small clearing. I stuck an arm out behind to warn Hawkins. He edged forward to stand beside me, Martha coming up on the other side.

A small building stood twenty yards away.

In daylight it probably looked picturesque and chocolate-box. At three in the morning, knowing what I knew, it seemed only grim and foreboding. Beside the house, two cars stood one behind the other. There were no lights anywhere. Beside me, Hawkins stiffened suddenly. Then he nudged me and pointed. I strained my eyes in the direction of his finger, closed them for a second, then opened them again. I learned that trick a long way from home, from an ageing sergeant who told me it had kept him alive through two wars. Now I could see it, a crumpled heap beside one of the cars, that could be a pile of old clothes, but we both knew it was a man's body.

'Got it,' I breathed. 'We cross the open ground from two sides, right?'

'Right,' he murmured. 'I'll go ten yards left, you take the right.'

I put my lips to Martha Chappel's ear.

'Stay where you are and don't breathe,' I whispered. 'If there's any trouble just run into the woods. Anywhere, but keep out of the way.'

She nodded. I eased cautiously past her, keeping in the protective shadows of the bushes ringing the clearing. When I judged I was far enough round, I stopped. Staring round at the silent foliage I tried to locate Hawkins and the girl, but could see nothing. It was probably less than twenty yards to the side of the cottage and I wasn't in such bad shape I'd need to rest on the way. But I'd seen the body near the cars, and it seemed long odds that the house was occupied. There were no lights, and that could mean whoever was in there was sitting at a black window waiting for some fool to try to cross the clear space. I swallowed and remembered how brave I was, but somehow my mouth was still dry. The .38 felt strong and friendly in my hand, but to be of any use it had to have something to point at. Without realising I'd reached a decision, I found myself all of a sudden bent double and heading for the house like a champion track man. Nothing happened. I crouched in the thin strip of darkness close by the wall, thin trickles of cold sweat running down my face. There was a blur of movement somewhere and I swung the gun hastily towards it. I just managed to freeze my finger on the trigger as I realised I was about to eliminate Hawkins. He came fast, head tucked in and made the house round the corner from me. Nobody tried to kill him either. All we had to do now was get together and work something out.

I edged cautiously along the wall on my haunches. When I reached the corner I stopped. It had just occurred to me that if Hawkins' nerves were as frayed as my own he might put a bullet in my head when I stuck it round the corner. Instead, I stuck out a tentative hand. When nobody blew a hole in it I gathered enough confidence to try looking round. There was a spot along the wall where the darkness seemed to intensify, and that had to be him. Easing cautiously round the corner I did my tortoise imitation towards him.

'What now?' he whispered.

I shook my head, then realised he wouldn't be able to see me. I whispered.

'Wait.'

The cars would have been left near the door of the house, that was fairly certain. That would make the door not more than fifteen feet along from where we were squatting. About five feet away, the man's body lay no more than an arm's length from the precious shadow thrown by the house. It seemed important to know who he was. That way we'd at least have some idea of who remained to be accounted for. I pushed Hawkins gently to get him moving. When we reached the spot near the body I tugged at his arm. We both stopped and stared at it. Stretching out an arm I slid it under the man to feel for his heart beat. He hadn't got a heart beat, and when I withdrew my hand it was sticky with blood. On an impulse I grabbed his head and lifted his face out of the dirt. It was Georgie Elman.

'Georgie Elman,' I whispered to Hawkins. 'He's dead.'

Hawkins grunted to let me know he understood.

'Now we make for the door. O.K.?' I asked.

Again I got that grunt, and we crept along towards where the door should be. Finally we saw it. It stood wide open, across a boarded porch and the black interior waited patiently. Suddenly Hawkins pulled my head towards him.

'Listen,' he muttered.

I listened and thought I heard something. A silence, then again the elusive sound. As my ears became attuned to it I tried to identify the sound. It was a low sobbing, half-wail, and it was being made by a human being. Whoever it was, was inside the house. The sound grew louder, and became unquestionably the eerie sound of a man weeping.

'You ready?' I asked.

By this time I was accustomed to the grunt. My mouth went dry again, and the sweat was pouring off my face. I crawled up on to the porch, Hawkins beside me every inch of the way. Then we got on our feet, and dived for the door. I went in first, tripped over something soft and flew headlong. Hawkins landed on top of me with crunching force, knocking the wind out of me. The unearthly sobbing was loud now as we scrambled quickly apart waiting for whatever happened next. Hawkins snapped suddenly.

'Who's there?'

There was no answer. I said,

'I'm going to try a flashlight, Hawkins. Don't shoot at it.'

'Right.'

I snapped on the pencil of light and probed quickly round the room. Bare walls stared back without interest then the beam lighted up Charles Augustin's face. He was sitting on the floor, back to the wall, and he was the one making the sound. His eyes were blank and he seemed oblivious to the sudden glare. I flicked around the rest of the room. Nobody was standing there with an axe waiting to bung it in my skull, and I was highly relieved. Beside the door I picked out a light switch.

'Let's try a real light,' I suggested.

Hawkins walked across and snapped down the switch. We both breathed with heavy relief, then saw what it was we'd tripped over. Cy Elman lay on his side, knees up and hands clutched at his middle where the blood was beginning to coagulate.

'Somebody took care of these two all right,' commented Hawkins.

There was no expression in his tone, no gladness, no pity, nothing. He was merely observing a fact.

'We'd better have a little talk with the hero,' he said next.

I nodded, and spoke to Charles Augustin.

'Augustin, up on your feet. The bad man went away.'

He didn't seem to hear. The handsome face was slack now, and he needed a shave. His mouth hung open foolishly, and the thin wailing came from between his lips with no conscious effort on his part. It was the eyes I didn't want to see. They had that curious opaque appearance which sometimes follows a seizure. I was certain he'd no idea we were there. I went across and knelt down beside him.

'Augustin, it's me, Preston,' I told him. 'Snap out of it.'

I could have saved my breath. Hawkins came to take a look.

'What do you make of it?' he asked. 'Think it's an act?'

'No,' I decided. 'I have seen this once before. A guy we found on a raft once with six others.

The six were all dead, and this guy had been alone with them for three days.'

'Dead,' repeated Augustin. 'All dead.'

'You see, he can hear all right,' snapped Hawkins suspiciously.

I didn't want to argue with him. In any case there wasn't time. Grabbing Charles by the shoulders I shook him hard. The sobbing noise stopped, but his face still looked empty.

'Can you hear me, Augustin?' I demanded.

Still nothing. I slapped him smartly across the cheek. He shook his head. I slapped him again, harder. This time he put a hand to his face and looked up at me. Something like anger appeared in his eyes.

'Get up,' I ordered.

He stared around as though wondering where he was. Then, putting a hand on the floor he levered himself upright.

'Preston?' he asked wonderingly.

'Yeah. What happened here?'

He paid no attention, but said instead,

'You hit me. It was you. You hit me. Why?'

'Because you were in some kind of shock. Never mind that now. What happened here tonight?'

'Here?' he still sounded uncertain.

'This is the cottage we're in,' I informed him. 'There are two dead men here. You

253

killed them. Why?'

Alarm came quickly to his face.

'Killed them? No, no it wasn't me.'

'Was it Avis?'

He grabbed quickly at my arm, and the alarm was now fear.

'Listen, you've got to stop her. She's insane. She'll butcher the whole town if she isn't stopped.'

'Where is she?' I demanded.

'She's not here,' he replied vaguely.

'I can see that. Where did she go?'

'She went. She's got a gun. You have to stop her, Preston.'

Hawkins interrupted.

'There's two cars outside, Augustin. One belongs to the Elmans. Is the other one yours?'

'Yes.'

'Did Mrs Augustin travel here with you?' he asked.

I was with him now.

'Yes, of course,' said Charles peevishly. 'We came together.'

If they'd come together, and there were still two cars outside, it could mean only one thing. She was out there somewhere, with a gun in her hand. And Martha Chappel was out there too.

'Mrs Chappel,' I snapped.

254

Hawkins was nearer to the door. He ran to it quickly.

'Mrs—'

A thunderous roar sounded from outside. Hawkins screamed and spun round, a great gout of blood pouring from his throat. His mouth was moving as though he wanted to tell me something. Then he waved his gun as though pushing something away. Now there was another shot. The impact of the heavy slug pushed him to his knees. He fell forward on his face and he was dead before he hit the floor. Charles shouted with fear. I smacked him across the face again.

'Hit the floor.'

Without waiting to see whether he obeyed or not, I made good time down there myself. From outside came a woman's laugh. I liked to hear a woman laugh, but heard across two corpses it was a chilling sound.

'Hey, Preston, that you in there?'

Avis sounded quite conversational. My own voice sounded like a croak.

'What do you want, Avis?'

'Listen, we don't want to fight,' she urged. 'Throw in with me and we'll say Charles did it.'

'You'll never get away with this,' I warned. 'Every cop in the state is looking for you right now.'

I was trying to guess the direction of the voice. One thing seemed reasonably certain. She hadn't found Martha Chappel. There would have been some sound. The situation wasn't too bad, so long as Avis didn't man-oeuvre herself into a position looking into the room from outside. That way she'd be able to pick me off like a clay pigeon. A clay pigeon that was lying on the ground. Charles Augustin spoke suddenly in a low voice.

'Do you think I'd be able to get to his gun?' he pointed at Hawkins' body.

'Not without me putting a slug in the back of your head,' I told him conversationally. 'From where I sit, you're on Avis's team, friend. She may scare you, but you're still her boy. Stay where you are.'

What happened next was nobody's fault but mine. I wasn't really paying more than half-attention to him. He'd been such a weak sister when I first arrived I hadn't any real apprecia-tion of the extent of his recovery. My main in-terest was to keep my attention riveted on the black square of the doorway, peering for any movement that could be the murderous Avis. I was lying forward, the .38 trained on the door-way. Augustin lay beside me, apparently in no condition to argue. Suddenly he lunged forward as he lay, his right hand knifing sharply against my wrist. The gun clattered to the wood floor. He rolled quickly, grabbed it and leaped to his feet.

'Avis,' he shouted excitedly. 'I've got the gun. It's all right. You can come in.'

There was no response from outside. He shouted a second time.

'Can you hear me, Avis? I've taken Preston's gun. He's unarmed.'

'You stinking little rat,' I told him.

If I had any chance to get out of there alive I had to get the .38 from Augustin. From what I'd seen I'd have no chance at all once Mrs Albert F Augustin got inside. I began to get up.

'Stay where you are,' said Charles hastily. 'Don't make me shoot. I will if I have to. Avis.'

He bellowed the name in something like desperation. I went on climbing to my feet, watching his eyes carefully.

'You're not going to use that, Charles,' I said softly. 'You don't have the stomach for it.'

'I warn you, Preston,' he stuttered. 'I'll kill you.'

There were only three feet between us. If I grabbed suddenly.

'Go on, Charles. Let's see you kill him.'

An amused voice spoke from the doorway.

I turned to see Avis standing there, and all hope died. Swinging loosely by her side was a blue automatic and I knew it would be another .38. The same one that killed Calvin Foyle.

The relief in Augustin's voice was pitiful.

'Avis,' he breathed gladly. 'I thought you'd never come.'

She chuckled, the same sound I'd heard back at Parkside Towers a million years ago. It had sounded different then.

'Go on, Charles, all you do is squeeze the trigger. It isn't difficult.'

He shook his head and pointed the gun at the floor.

'You know I can't kill someone in cold blood.'

'Huh,' she sneered. 'All my life I picked nothing but losers. Even now.'

'You're not going to get away with this,' I warned her.

She looked at me thoughtfully.

'You don't think so? Oh, I see what you mean. You're counting this chicken in it.'

She pointed at Charles who flushed.

'He won't last ten minutes against any questioning. You're practically in the gas chamber right now,' I told her.

'With him in it I agree with you,' she nodded. 'So why don't we leave him out? You and me together, that would be something.'

'Yeah,' I agreed. 'Until you thought I'd been around too long. I'd wake up one morning to find I was dead.'

'Nobody lives forever,' she shrugged. 'It's a better deal than what's going to happen to you now.'

I pretended to consider.

'How would we explain this battlefield here?'

'Listen, you can't talk to him this way as though I'm not here,' protested Charles suddenly.

'Oh, shut up. I was going to have to get rid of you sometime anyway. You're no use to me any more.'

It was amazing that she could speak to him that way. He had a gun in his hand, but she paid it no attention. She evidently thought she could do as she liked with Charles, gun or no gun. And from the abject way he stood there staring dejectedly at the floor, it seemed she might be right.

'She's going to kill you, Charles. She's going to kill both of us, and let you take the rap for all this. Use the gun.'

She laughed, and it froze me.

'You got plenty nerve, Preston. It's a pity we couldn't get along.'

I knew from her tone this was the time. The

light reflected coldly from the blue steel as she swung the automatic up towards me. The explosion was terrific. I waited for the searing agony at my middle. Instead, Avis Augustin pitched forward and lay still. Her back was a ragged horror of blood. Martha Chappel stood in the doorway, cuddling the big shotgun I'd seen at the house. So that was why she'd been walking so stiffy. She'd had the thing tucked under her coat the whole time.

'Give Mr Preston the gun, Charles,' she ordered crisply.

Dully he handed it over, then dropped to his knees beside Avis. A tear rolled down his face.

'Not dead,' he croaked in disbelief. 'She can't be dead. Not Avis.'

He lookd up at me pleadingly. I felt repelled.

'Thanks,' I said to Martha.

I should have said more, much more, but right then I was choked with relief and dispersing fear. Martha swayed, and the gun waved dangerously.

'Sorry,' she muttered. 'I've—I've never—'

I ran to catch her as she started to faint.

'Get some water,' I told Charles.

He nodded anxiously, glad to be told what to do. Glad he was alive. Everything was going to be all right, so long as he got that water. So long as he did exactly what everybody told him. This whole business had been none of his doing. It wasn't him, not Charles Augustin. It had been those others, the bad ones.

Now he hurried up with a dirty cup filled with water. I held it against Martha's lips.

'Here, drink a little of this.'

Her eyes fluttered and she sipped. Then she coughed, shook her head and stood upright. Her face was puzzled.

'Did I faint?' she asked. 'It's not like me. I've never done it before.'

I grinned.

'Mrs Chappel, you're all right. You've prevented a murder, maybe two. As for what you did, don't let your mind dwell on it.'

I pointed to what had recently been Avis Augustin.

'When you hear the whole story about this, you won't even think you did anything but a social service.'

Before we left I checked Frank Hawkins' body. There was no doubt he was quite dead. The place was like a slaughterhouse. To Charles I said,

'Take your sister out to the car. Make one wrong move, even look sideways and I'll kill you. It won't mean a thing to me, pal. I'll squash you like a fly.'

I said it as if I meant it. I probably did mean it, but I knew it wouldn't be put to the test. There was nothing left in Charles. He offered Martha his arm but she pushed it away, and together they went out. I went back to Hawkins' body and felt in his inside pockets. There was a wallet with a picture of a young man who could have passed for a more sensitive Hawkins in his younger days. There was money too, almost seven hundred dollars. I took the money and the picture and replaced the wallet. Then I remembered how thorough Rourke's boys always were. I removed the wallet again, wiped it very carefully with a handkerchief and put it back a second time. After a last look round I went back out to the car. There didn't seem to be any point to switching off the light.

CHAPTER 18

Back at the house, we walked dejectedly through the great doors.

'You seem to be in charge, Mr Preston,' Martha told me. 'Shall I call the police now?'

'Not for a while.' I shook my head. 'They'll be here too soon. There are one or two things

I have to know first. Once the boys from the department get here, none of us will get any peace. The sensible thing is to get ready for the ordeal. Can you rustle up some coffee?'

She nodded.

'If you think it's all right. I mean about not calling right away.'

'It isn't all right,' I admitted. 'There's a man named Rourke, Lieutenant Rourke, and he'll probably play hell if he finds we held out on him for a whole half-hour. But believe me, you'll be thankful for thirty minutes comparative peace and some coffee before we let the whole town in.'

She didn't argue any more, but went away towards the back of the house, Charles stood waiting for me to tell him what to do.

'In there,' I snapped.

We went into the room where Hawkins and I had our talk with Martha Chappel a couple of hours before. Now Hawkins was dead, Avis was dead, and the only person I knew who could tell me why was Charles Augustin.

'Sit down. We're going to talk,' I explained. 'I am going to ask questions and you are going to answer them. Give me any trouble and I'll put a bullet in your leg. I'll tell the police you tried to make a break. Got it?'

To give the word emphasis. I took out the

.38 and rested it on the arm of my chair. He watched me, with fear in his eyes.

'I know some of it. You're going to tell me the rest,' I informed him. 'Frank Hawkins was bringing the stuff in. Right?'

'Yes.'

'The stuff was heroin. Frank delivered to you, Avis and the Elmans. How did that come about?'

He curled his lip.

'Mostly as a result of my father's generosity. If he hadn't kept me so short of money, I would never have become involved in such a thing.'

'It was Avis' idea?' I prompted.

'Absolutely. The money he gave her was hardly enough to pay her hair stylist. Well she had this idea. She knew one or two people, so she told me. All we needed to get into the set-up was the first lot of stake-money. That would pay for our first shipment. This we would sell at a fat profit, and after that it would all be easy.'

'Sounds all right,' I commented. 'What went wrong?'

'Nothing,' he replied. 'We could have gone on with it for ever.'

'I'll come back to that in a minute. Where did you raise the stake money to buy in?'

He sighed.

'That was the only reason Avis let me in on it at all. I passed a few cheques with my father's signature on them. Not one big one. That would have caused comment before I got the money. I made out a number for smaller amounts and raised the money that way.'

'But you knew you'd never get away with that,' I objected. 'A big name like your father, he would have had regular checks with the bank to ensure nothing like this was happening.'

'You're absolutely right. There was no suggestion that I'd get away with it. The point was, I could raise the necessary money before my father discovered what was going on. When he did, which was within less than two days, he sent for me. There was a great showdown that morning, but I'd gambled on the result, and I won. I was certain he'd never take action against me. Not legal action, that is. All it amounted to was a lot of shouting and accusations, but he wasn't going to do anything.'

I had to work at it to keep the disgust out of my voice.

'So you and Avis got the money. Just now, you said the import business could have gone on for ever. What happened to prevent it?'

He rubbed at the back of his hand impatiently.

'It went along fine for a long time. Must have been most of two years. We were getting two, three shipments a year, and averaging about twenty thousand profit each time. It wasn't the pot of gold, but I was satisfied, so were the Elmans.'

'But Avis got greedy,' I murmured, more to myself than Augustin.

'How about the Elmans? You didn't meet them at the country club, I imagine?'

'No. I put up the money, Avis the ideas. But we weren't in touch with the market and the Elmans were. Avis had known them before, somewhere else, and it was her suggestion we bring them in. They were pigs.'

'They're dead pigs now,' I reminded him. 'Avis wasn't satisfied with the take, so she got some new scheme. What was it?'

'She wanted to take a shipment without paying for it. That way we'd made the greater part of two hundred thousand dollars at one hit. Half for the Elmans, half for us. There was only one snag, the courier.'

'Nielson,' I muttered. 'You'd have to kill him.'

'Yes. I didn't want any part of it. What we were doing was bad, all right it was plain rotten if you prefer it, but I couldn't go for murder.'

Curious sets of values people have. Augustin hadn't any qualms about helping and encouraging hundreds, maybe thousands, of people to take narcotics. An evil and insidious habit that can only have one ultimate conclusion. But he shrank from the more direct act of taking one human life.

'What about the Elmans? They were pros. They'd know the big boys would never stand for it, and there would be professional killers on the job at once. Don't tell me they liked the scheme.'

'Not at first,' he admitted. 'But you didn't know Avis. She had a kind of genius for evil. Not two brains in her head for anything worthwhile, but anything crooked seemed to give her inspiration. Her plan was to put the blame on the courier, Nielson. She said if we took the stuff, then killed him and got rid of the body completely, we could then pass back a message that he'd taken our money and kept the stuff. We could even send threats about what we'd do if our money wasn't made good.'

'Who killed Nielson?' I queried.

'I'm coming to that. We always met him at the Beano Club. Avis would book a private room, and the whole thing would take about ten minutes. Avis wanted to take care of Nielson personally. She said she couldn't trust any of the rest of us to do it properly. And she was going to do it without witnesses. She didn't propose to spend the rest of her life paying out blackmail money to me or the Elman brothers.'

'Avis thought of everything,' I commented.

'Oh, yes,' he agreed.'As I said, she had a pure criminal mind. On the night this was to happen, Nielson arrived on schedule. He'd made the same deal with us a dozen times and he had no reason to suspect us. As he walked into the room, Cy Elman hit him on the head, and injected some heroin into him to keep him under. He and his brother took the dope, that was their part finished. After they left, I went too.'

'How was Avis supposed to get rid of the guy single-handed?'

'That was her part of it, and she wouldn't answer any questions. The manager, Foyle, he'd have a part in it somewhere, I was sure of that. He was crazy about her, like plenty of other people.'

We were interrupted by Martha Chappel. She came in carrying a tray full of coffee. It went down like the finest brandy. She stood around uncertainly.

'Do you want me here, Mr Preston? I can easily go—'

'Please stay, Mrs Chappel. You won't like what you hear, but you'd better have it now at first-hand. The courtroom will come later.'

She was pale, but had herself under control. It was noticeable that she couldn't bring herself to look at her brother, and sat as far away from him as she could get. Augustin protested.

'Is this necessary? Surely there's no need for Martha—?'

'Shut up,' I clipped. 'There wasn't any need for anything that's happened these past few days. You blame everything on Avis if you want, but she couldn't operate without people, and you were one of them. Maybe the worst one. If you're concerned about your sister's sensibilities, you could have started thinking about those years ago. After what she's been through tonight, I don't imagine there's anything you're going to say that will shock her in the least. That is, if you can stand any more, Mrs Chappel?'

She nodded grimly.

'I'll stay. My opinion of my brother hasn't exactly been high for ten years or more. I might as well know it all before I read it in the papers.'

I felt sorry for her. She was the only one in the whole rotten mess who deserved any sympathy at all. I got back to Charles.

269

'You were saying you walked out and left Avis to take care of Nielson. What happened?'

He glanced at his sister worriedly, but she refused to look at him. 'This man Nielson was as strong as a horse. We all thought he was completely unconscious, but somehow he pulled himself together enough to take Avis by surprise. She thought he was going to kill her, but he had no intention of doing that. He said the organisation would take care of her when they were ready. And the rest of us too. He told her he wouldn't do her any harm. She was already dead, and now she could just walk around waiting for the executioners to catch up with her. He wanted the money, and when he found she hadn't got it, he said he was sure my father would be glad to pay it to keep his son and his wife out of jail. Then he left.'

'Did he go to your father?'

'Yes, I think he must have. Not that night, though. Later my father made it plain he knew what was going on, and it could only have been Nielson that told him.'

'All right. After Nielson left, what did Avis do?'

'Could I have a cigarette?'

I tossed him a pack of Old Favourites and he lit it with trembling hands. I tried one too but it tasted sour and bitter on my tongue, so I crushed it out.

'What did Avis do after she let Nielson get away?' I pressed.'

'She had a few moments of panic, then she started thinking again. The first thing to do was get home here. If Nielson came straight to my father she might still have a chance to—er—carry out the original plan.'

I turned to Martha Chappel.

'The original plan,' I mimicked Charles' tone, 'was to murder the aforementioned Nielson.' Then to Charles, 'All right, so she came home.'

'No,' he contradicted. 'That was where she had this bad luck. Some drunken kid had stolen the car, father's car, and killed himself. The police were on the spot at once, and of course Avis realised they might ask why she'd wanted a private room. So she made Foyle tell them it was my father who'd made the reservation. Then she telephoned here and told my father what happened to the car. She told him she'd been there with a man, and if he didn't want that in every newspaper in the state next morning, he'd better say he'd used the room for a business meeting. Nobody would query anything he said.'

'And your father agreed?' I asked. It sounded unlikely to me.

Charles said in a flat tone.

'He agreed. I didn't know it at the time, but he'd had to cover up for Avis on one or two occasions in the past.'

'I can vouch for the truth of that,' Martha butted in. 'My father's late and unlamented wife was as pretty a slut as you'd find in a day's march.'

For somebody unaccustomed to violence, Martha Chappel was bearing up remarkably well. I wondered fleetingly whether she'd have stood up to the night's events with quite such fortitude if the person she'd been driven to kill had been someone other than Avis Augustin.

'Your story sounds all right up to now,' I told Charles. 'But all this happened a couple of months back. What happened to make everything blow up in the past three days?'

He looked dejected.

'My father's death, among other things. Your interference didn't help matters either. You see, we had all this money, or at least I thought we had. The money wasn't the foremost thing in our minds at first. We kept waiting for Nielson to move. He'd been in touch with my father and told him what we were mixed up in. The old man didn't believe it, but he sent for me and had it out. I never could stand up to him. He got the whole story

out of me, made me sign a paper, a kind of con-
fession. He also had a private firm checking on
Avis' movements. He'd always known what
she was, and she'd never made any secret of
it, but now he started preparing a proper
dossier on her. Then there was this trouble with
the Elmans.'

'What kind of trouble?'

'They double-crossed us. They simply walked out with the stuff that night, and they never
intended to pay us our share. As they said, it
was the last delivery we'd ever get. Even if the
big people in Hong Kong believed our story
about Nielson, they'd certainly never do business with us again. That's the way they work.
They never run the slightest risk. So the Elmans decided there was no point in handing
over our share. We couldn't exactly sue them,
could we?'

'Not quite. So what was Avis going to do
about them?'

'Avis never told anybody what was in her
mind. It was only very recently the Elmans told
us they proposed to cut us out. A few days later
you came into the picture, and that gave her
an idea. She told them you were investigating
a narcotics tip, and you could be dangerous.'

And that would account for my little encounter in the alley with the steel cutters.

Something else I could thank Avis for.

'She had an inventive turn of mind, our Avis. Did she kill your father, or was that your contribution?'

Martha drew in her breath quickly and looked across at Charles.

'No,' he denied vehemently. 'No, that was a terrible shock to me.'

'And to Avis, I imagine,' I said.

'Not exactly. Nothing was a shock to her. No, Preston, you can believe it or not, as you wish, but my father killed himself.'

'Why would he do that?'

'He'd been getting more and more depressed for some time. He knew what we'd been doing and that hardly helped him feel any better. Then, that morning, he came home unexpectedly. He—he found us. Found Avis and me.'

Disgust was written large on Martha Chappel's face.

'You couldn't even spare him that, could you?'

'We weren't to know. He left the office early, and that was most unusual.'

'You say he found you,' I interrupted. 'It doesn't figure. I saw you out on the grass myself. It might have made him furious, but it wouldn't cause him to blow his brains out.'

Charles grimaced.

'He didn't find us there. We were—upstairs.'

'Upstairs,' echoed Martha. 'You mean you were both in bed and he caught you?'

'Yes.' Even Charles contrived to look shame-faced. 'He stood and looked at us without saying anything. Then Avis laughed. She taunted him with it. He turned around and went downstairs. Next thing we heard was the shot. We rushed down and found him. We were both dumbstruck. As we stood there looking at him, we heard a car pull up outside. Your car, Preston. Avis did some of her famous quick thinking and we were out on that grass in a clinch when you arrived. The rest you know.'

'Kind of elaborate, wasn't it?' I demanded. 'All you had to do was call the police.'

'I could see that later,' he agreed. 'But when you have a load of guilt on your mind you don't tend to think like honest people. Nothing would have convinced either of us to call the police voluntarily. Avis was afraid one of us would be blamed for killing him, and I was so confused I agreed with her. I always agreed with Avis.'

Martha Chappel offered more coffee and I accepted thankfully. Between sips I said to Charles,

'After that everything seemed to go wrong
275

at once, huh? That phoney stunt you pulled hiding the gun, that was crazy. The police didn't like it.'

'That was my own idea,' he confessed. 'It was a sort of double bluff. I knew the police would find out the truth quickly. I knew they wouldn't think highly of me, but at least it would clear me of any suspicion in their minds. I thought it was a brilliant idea. Till later that is.'

'Why was Foyle killed?'

'That was his own fault. He didn't deserve any better. After you went to see him he contacted me and demanded money. Said he'd tell you what he knew if I didn't pay up by that evening. I told Avis, and she said she'd take care of it.'

'She took care of it all right,' I confirmed. 'And almost managed to get me arrested for it. We can't waste any more time on this. Tell us about tonight.'

He put his face in his hands and shuddered.

'Tonight was awful. Avis had told Cy Elman she'e level the score with him. He telephoned me and told me I'd better change her mind or he and his brother would be looking for both of us. It was just after I'd left police headquarters. I couldn't locate Avis for a while, then I thought she'd gone off on a bend. She'd do

that sometimes, when she felt like it. Finally,
I ran her down in a bar—'

'—Sam's Place,' I muttered, half to myself.

'How did you know that?'

'It doesn't matter. Then what?'

'I told her I couldn't go back to the house
because Martha had thrown me out. We didn't
want to go to a hotel, because there was too
much chance they would find us. You see it
wasn't only the Elmans now. The other people
were in town, the ones Nielson had threatened us with.'

'How did you know that?' I butted in.

'From Foyle. Also the Elmans had told me
earlier. This man had been to see them and
they'd sworn to him they knew nothing about
it. They told him they were just small fry, and
Avis and I handled all the business end. They
told this man I forget his name—'

'—Powell,' I contributed. 'His name is
Kingsland Powell.'

Charles was all through looking surprised.
He merely accepted the name.

'Yes, that was it, Powell. The Elmans told
Powell the story we'd agreed, that Nielson had
robbed us. But they added they only had the
story from Avis and me. They advised me to
find a hundred and fifty thousand for Powell or
start praying. Well, I had no chance of raising

a sum like that.'

'How about Avis? She must have had plenty stacked away.'

'No. Avis had a lot of weaknesses, and the worst was gambling. Her share of whatever we made was always gone in a few days. All she had was a few thousand, and that wasn't going to buy off Powell. He'd want it all.'

'And that was when you asked your sister for the money?' I suggested.

'It was. Naturally, she refused.'

Martha said dully,

'I hadn't got anything like that amount. But I would have refused in any case. And I would have been right.'

'Thank you for the sermon, sister dear,' snapped Charles. 'I hope you're satisfied with the results.'

'You can cut that right out,' I threatened. 'You're just here to answer questions. Nothing else. So by the end of the day you had Powell on your tail, and you also figured the Elmans would be after you, too. What did you do?'

He glared at me but it was just for show. There wasn't any fight in him.

'As I already told you, we couldn't risk a public place. It's too easy for a determined man to trace anyone. You should know that, in your business. So we thought of the cottage.'

'How did the Elmans know about that place?' I queried.

'I had no idea they knew it. Wild horses wouldn't have dragged me there if I'd suspected for a moment they'd know about it. When we heard on the radio the police were looking for them I got really frightened.'

I laughed. Martha said,

'I don't see the joke, Mr Preston.'

'The Elmans,' I explained. 'Somebody tipped off the law about where to find them. When the police got there the place was stiff with junk—er that is, heroin. They must have thought it was Avis turned them in, as a reprisal.'

'And wasn't it?' she asked.

'No. It was me. I just wanted them locked up for a few hours. I'd no idea the police would find what they did.'

Charles looked at me oddly, and said,

'I wish I'd known that. When Avis heard the newscast, it was the first time I'd ever seen her frightened. She said they'd be bound to think she was responsible. Till then, she hadn't taken very seriously my suggestion that we might be in real danger. She told me Cy Elman knew about the cottage. They'd discussed the place once as a possible clearing house for the dope, but finally decided against it. So when Cy and

Georgie arrived, Avis was ready for them. And you saw the result.'

'Yeah,' I said shortly. 'We saw the result. Well, all your troubles are over, Augustin. In a few months you'll sit in that little glass room and the State will supply the dope. Time for the police now, Mrs Chappel.'

She nodded and went out to the telephone. 'Which is Avis' room?' I asked Charles. 'It's upstairs. Third door on the right.'

I went out into the hall. Martha looked at me enquiringly over the telephone. I went upstairs, found the door and went in. It was a hotch-potch of pieces of good furniture plus the kind of thing I would have expected somebody like Avis to acquire. There were some pieces of good jewellery in a leather box but that wasn't what I wanted. I searched quickly around. The floor of the wardrobe was a mess of expensive shoes, heaped up anyhow. I raked around among them and came up with a flat cardboard box. I took a deep breath and opened it. Inside were rows of hundred dollar bills. There was no time to count them, but I knew there'd be close to a hundred and fifty thousand dollars in all.

Indecision gnawed briefly. Whose money was it? Charles had stolen it from his father originally, but the father was dead. Avis had murdered for it, but she was gone too. Hundreds of unfortunate addicts had contributed their twenties and fifties, but they'd never seen them again. The only legitimate owners were Kingsland Powell's employers in Hong Kong. They had supplied merchandise which had never been paid for. But when I thought about the nature of the stuff, and its equivalent value in human misery, I couldn't burst into tears about the legitimacy of their claim. It seemed to me the heir of the original owner had as good a right as anybody. But not all of it. I'd been sticking out my neck all over town for the past few days, and all for two hundred dollars. I wasn't going to get any more from my deceased client, that was a certainty.

I weighed the box of bills thoughtfully in my hands. Nobody would ever know if I stole the lot. Then I sighed and thought of all the nights I wouldn't sleep, worrying about it. The money was owed to Hong Kong Narcotics Ltd, or whatever. They were willing to pay ten thousand dollars by way of a reward. I figured Martha Chappel had a better right to it, but on the other hand she didn't even know the money existed, I lifted out two packets of the bills, roughly a hundred as near as I could estimate. These I slipped inside my coat. If Martha Chappel was to have the money, she at least ought to pay the same reward as the competition.

Downstairs she was waiting for me.

'The police are on their way,' she informed me. She looked curiously at the box in my hand but didn't ask any questions.

'You'd better have this, Mrs Chappel.'

Silently she took it from me, looked inside. 'I don't understand.'

I told her where I'd found the money.

'Avis just couldn't play fair with anybody. She knew if Charles suspected she had the money, he'd find some way to get his hands on it. So she told him all that stuff about big gambling losses. If your brother knew anything about real gamblers, the compulsive kind, he would have known Avis wasn't the type.'

'I see. You're a strange man, Mr Preston. Why are you handing all this money over to me?'

'It's yours, the way I see it, Charles swindled your father out of it years ago, and your father left everything to you.'

'I can think of plenty of people who might have forgotten to mention it, if they found a sum like this.'

'Yeah,' I agreed. 'I thought about that. But it wouldn't be any benefit to me if I hung on to it. To you it's just money. You've always been accustomed to plenty of it, and this won't change you in any way. I'm different. I have low tastes, Mrs Chappel. For me, that dough would be nothing more than a one way ticket to the skids. As I am, I get bouts of low life when the money situation permits it. They're just episodes, and they help to balance me out. It's more normal that way.'

She managed a small smile.

'If you say so. And thank you.'

It sounded like a cannon going off in the room behind us. She went white.

'Oh, my God,' she whispered.

I ran for the door and threw it wide. Charles Augustin was sitting in a chair, the shotgun between his knees, barrel towards his head. He was rocking back and forth, tears streaming down his face. The flying dust and the sharp stench of cordite made me cough. Behind me his sister stood looking at him.

'What happened?' she asked, voice shaking.

I walked across to Charles and pulled the gun away from him. There was a great hole in the ceiling above his head.

'Pull yourself together,' I roared.

He shook his head and sobbed.

'Did he try to—to kill himself?' asked Martha.

'Him?' I filled my voice with contempt. 'Kill

himself? No. That takes a certain amount of guts. He doesn't have any. He set it up all right, then chickened out at the last second.'

Outside, in the breaking dawn, the unearthly wail of a police siren shattered the quiet.

CHAPTER 19

At five the following afternoon I sat steaming in the car watching a certain store front. Beside me, Sam Thompson fell asleep for the third time in ten minutes. I jabbed him irritably in the ribs.

'Wassat for?' he grumbled, heaving himself straight. 'Nobody's asleep.'

I grunted and went on staring out of the window. It had been one hell of a day. Rourke had gone easy on me for once. I think he was so pleased to have Charles Augustin in custody, he wasn't going to be too hard on the man who brought it about. But everything else had been terrible. The questions, the lack of sleep, the whole bit. Only one incident had given a little light relief. I'd been sitting in Rourke's office, more asleep that awake, in between quiz sessions. Schultz had come for me.

'There's a guy just been caught trying to get into that warehouse of the Elman boys. He swears he's just an insurance salesman, but he makes like a phoney to me. Plus he's carrying a gun.'

'Really?' I wasn't very interested. 'A pusher, maybe?'

Schultz shrugged.

'Who knows. You seem to know most every crook on the coast. Come take a look at him. He may fit in this caper somewhere, and you may have come against him.'

Wearily I shuffled after the temporary sergeant down to the interrogation room. There was a man sitting with his back to me. Standing either side, a couple of plain-clothes men shot alternate questions at him. As we walked in they knocked it off, looking at me curiously.

'This is the guy,' snapped Schultz, now all brisk authority. 'Can you place him in this heroin smuggling?'

I walked around to look at the man. Kingsland Powell stared up at me blandly.

'No,' I began, 'I don't think—Wait a minute.'

I looked at him harder. A muscle twitched at his throat, but otherwise his calm was undisturbed.

'Yes,' I said thoughtfully. 'I think so. Yes,

this is the man.'

Schultz was triumphant in a quiet way.

'Take your time, Preston. We don't want any hurried identification.'

'This isn't one,' I assured him. 'I place this guy now.'

'I see. Tell us about it, will you? The whole thing.'

Powell's eyes narrowed very slightly, and they never left my face.

'He came to see me at my apartment a few days ago.'

'Ah,' breathed Schultz. 'What about?'

'Insurance,' I returned carefully. 'He wanted to sell me a policy.'

One of the detectives sighed. Schultz said hoarsely.

'You mean that's the only way you remember him, some insurance deal?'

'Yes.'

'He doesn't come into this other matter at all?'

Not unless his company carries the cover on any of those people out at the Augustin place last night.'

Powell spoke now.

'I've been trying to recall where we met Mr—er, Mr Pretlove?'

'Preston,' I corrected.

A relieved smile came over his face.

'Of course, of course. Mr Preston. The private detective, isn't it? I remember what a very nice place you had. Oh, yes, I have it now.'

'This isn't a social club,' Schultz became officious. 'Did you buy any insurance, Preston?'

'No. I have some good cover already. Anyhow this man's company—er—what was it again—?'

'—Eastern Waters Mutual Fidelity,' supplied Powell eagerly.

'—that was it,' I nodded. 'The premiums were just this side of extortion.'

Powell got angry.

'That remark, sir, is little short of slanderous. I advise you to watch your tongue.'

'Look,' I replied nastily. 'I told you what I thought of your company the other night. The figures you quoted were ridiculous.'

'Nothing of the kind,' he said snappishly. 'Remember your occupation, Mr Preston. A hazardous calling to say the least. As I recall I quoted—'

'Never mind what you quoted,' roared Schultz. 'You want to talk business, go rent an officer. You Preston, outside.'

As I left, I cut off everyone else's view of Powell's face. He grinned quickly and winked.

That was the last time I ever saw him.

Thompson grunted suddenly and interrupted my thoughts.

'That's her,' he pointed.

I looked at the pretty girl who was emerging from the store across the street.

'O.K, Sam, thanks. I'll mail you some dough.'

He climbed out.

'Never mind the mail,' he told me. 'Leave it with Florence. I'll be around tomorrow to collect.'

I nodded and eased off the brake. She walked with a supple, swinging stride, an appealing sight in her bright yellow dress with the red shoes. All at once she began to run, and a crosstown bus swung past me to a halt at the stop up ahead. I played chase with the bus through the now heavy business traffic, which thinned gradually as we hit the edge of town. Finally the bus reached its destination, a small clutter of white-painted buildings, and pulled up. The doors swung smoothly back, and the girl in the yellow dress stepped down daintily. At once a slim boy materialised from a garage, fifty yards away. He covered the distance in seconds, stopped when he reached her and took her hand. They smiled into each other's eyes, and I felt quick envy for the boy. Now I rolled along the kerb beside them, braked and climbed out. They took no notice at all. I doubt whether they even knew I was there.

'Hallo,' I said. 'Could I talk to you for a minute?'

They looked around, startled. The boy asked,

'What about? I don't know you. Do you, Sue?'

She shook her head.

'No. I never saw him before.'

'But I know you,' I informed her gently. 'You're Susan Hofmeyer. And I want to talk about this.'

I pulled from my pocket the folded mid-day edition of the *Globe*. They looked at the thick headlines on the lead story. Susan blanched slightly.

'Who are you?' demanded the mechanic.

'The name is Preston. The villainous looking picture in column three, that's me.'

He looked at the picture, then back to the original. His shoulders slumped.

'Where do you want to talk?'

'Preferably somewhere we could sit down,' I suggested.

'C'mon.'

Susan hung on to his arm tight as he made his way around the side of the garage. She

289

wouldn't look at me. We came to a small square of grass with a table and four cane chairs perched in the middle. The boy sat down and stared doggedly at his hands. Susan Hofmeyer moved her chair close to him, and that left me in opposition to both of them. I sat, and laid the newspaper on the table.

'You've led me a fine chase, Jeff,' I remarked.

He said nothing, but continued to study the oil-stained hands. I waited. Finally he spoke, in a flat lifeless tone.

'Will I be arrested?'

'What for? Did you do something?'

The reply seemed to surprise him. Enough, at least, to make him look over at me.

'What do you want? If it's money, you have the wrong address.'

I shook my head.

'Not money. Information. I want to know how it happened. Your brother Frank paid me to find out what happened to you.'

There was quick pain in his eyes at the mention of Frank's name.

'You were there, huh? Did he—did he suffer much?'

'Never knew what hit him,' I assured him. 'He died quickly and cleanly. That's the truth.'

He nodded.

'I believe you. Well, what exactly can I tell you? According to what I read, you were in on every move. All my information is strictly second-hand from the newspapers.'

'No,' I contradicted. 'I don't know the start of it. The end, yes. I could probably tell you a lot about that. But the beginning, that was yours.'

'Yes.'

He turned to the girl and pressed her hand gently. She smiled uncertainly.

'Might as well, honey,' he said. 'This man knows who I am anyhow. Nothing will make any difference now.'

I avoided looking at them, and made a great show of extracting an Old Favourite from my pack and lighting it.

'You knew about Frank?' he demanded suddenly.

'Not at first. At first he was just what he said, a man whose brother had been killed. He hired me to investigate the circumstances.'

'I see. You probably don't know how it was with Frank and me. He was several years older, and practically raised me. To me he was the greatest guy on earth. Always helping me, encouraging, putting me back on the track if I looked like wandering off. That was before I found out what he was doing.'

'How did you find out?'

'I always knew exactly when he was due home from a trip. But he never came straight to our apartment. There was always some business he had to do first. I accepted it, naturally. Why should I question what my own brother was doing? Then one time, six months ago or more I was in town when I saw Frank in the distance. I knew his ship was due, so I wasn't especially surprised to see him. I went after him, but there were plenty of people around and I couldn't get through the crowds. After a while I got curious about where he was going. I followed him. He went to a house in a quiet part of town, went inside and stayed there. I got tired of waiting so I went home. When he arrived later, he told me he'd been on his usual business since the ship docked. That puzzled me, because I couldn't see what business he'd have in an ordinary private house. After a few days Frank went to sea again. You probably think I was pretty nosy, but Frank and me, we only had each other. We didn't have separate lives, not really. So I couldn't get this out of my head. Finally I got so curious, I found out who lived in the house.'

'A man named Nielson?' I hazarded.

'How could you possibly know that?' he asked in surprise.'

'I know the end,' I reminded him.

'Sure. Well, I got interested in this Nielson. He didn't do any work, that I could see. He had a fine house, big car, lived in style in an unassuming kind of way. But nobody seemed to know anything about him at all. The next time the *Star of Monkton*, that was Frank's ship, next time she docked, I was waiting to follow Frank. It was the same performance again. He went straight to Nielson's house. I was ready this time. I'd left a note telling Frank I'd be home late. It was evening when Frank got to Nielson's. I spied on them.'

He flushed as he said it, and even after all that had happened, Jeff Hawkins was obviously ashamed to admit he'd spied on his brother.'

'They went into a room at the side of the house. I watched through the window. Frank gave the man a package. He opened it, I couldn't see what was inside. After he'd looked, he took the package away. Then he came back and gave Frank money. They shook hands and Frank left the house. I guessed by this time Frank was smuggling, but I didn't know exactly what. I had my old convertible down the street. I went and sat in it and waited.

After about an hour Nielson got his car from the garage and drove away. I followed him. We went out to the Beano Club. Nielson went inside. I'd been there once or twice, and I knew he was heading for the private rooms at the back. I was getting used to being underhanded by that time. I went around and watched through the window.'

'Nobody saw you round there?' I interjected.

'No. I was afraid one of the kitchen staff might come out for a smoke or something, but I was lucky.'

I dropped my cigarette on the grass and ground it out with great care.

'Who was in the room, besides Nielson?' I questioned.

'There was this society woman, Mrs Augustin Senior, I knew her from the Oyster's Cloister.'

'That creature,' said Susan viciously.

Jeff managed a wry grin.

'Susan doesn't mean because of what happened last night,' he explained. 'Mrs Augustin got high one night at the Cloister and she—er—well, she suggested—'

'I have the picture,' I helped him out. 'I know all about the lady.'

'Some lady,' sniffed Susan.

'She was there,' I prompted. 'Anybody else?'

'Two other men. I didn't know them then,

but I didn't like the look of either one. Later I found out their names. Cyrus and George Elman. As I say, Nielson was there. He handed the package to these people. The men examined it, the same way Nielson had when Frank gave it to him. Then they nodded to Mrs Augustin and she handed over a whole stack of money. Nielson checked it very quickly, put it in a bag, and left.'

'What did you do then?'

'I didn't know what to do at first, whether to follow Nielson or not. I decided not. After all, I knew where he lived and had already learned all I could about him. So I hung around, waiting for the other two to come out. The men that is,' he added, with a sly look at Susan.'

She made a face at him. I reminded them I wasn't there to watch games.

'You followed the men, huh?'

'Yes. They went to a store in Monkton. They obviously lived there, they had keys and all. So now I knew who everybody was. All I didn't know was what all of this had to do with my brother Frank. I thought he must be in some kind of trouble, bad trouble for him not to tell me about it. After he went off again, I had a systematic campaign finding out all I could about the Elmans. If there's anything good to

295

know about them, I never heard it. I didn't care what their rotten racket was with Nielson and the Augustin woman. My only concern was what it had to do with Frank, and how to help him out of the mess. He was only on a short run, and I decided to have it out with him when he got back. Things didn't work out the way I'd hoped.'

'They never do,' I consoled.

There was bitterness in his voice now and it was almost as though my presence no longer meant anything. He was thinking out loud, rather than talking to me.

'The day he was due, I had a cable from him. Said he was shipping out again within a matter of hours. There was a lot of sickness among the officers in the shipping line, and Frank had to pinch-hit for one of them in another ship. It meant he would have very little time ashore, and if he missed me this trip we'd make it up next time. This had happened before, a couple of years ago, so I wasn't all that surprised. But I was annoyed, because it meant we couldn't have our showdown. I wanted to know whether he'd be finding time to pay a call on Nielson, so I went and waited near the house as soon as the ship docked. Frank turned up all right. I didn't go to the house this time. I didn't imagine the performance would be any different.

When Frank came out he saw the car and got inside. He wanted to know what I was doing there, and when I told him he got mad. I'd never seen him so mad. I said if he was in trouble, all I wanted was to help him out. Then he nearly took off. He didn't need any nursemaid, he told me. He'd do what the hell he pleased and who did I think I was sticking my nose into his business. I talked up then, and told him what I thought about what he was doing and the people he was mixed up with. We had plenty to say to each other. Finally Frank told me to keep out of it. Nielson and the others would kill if they had to, and the fact I was Frank's brother wouldn't mean a thing. He told me I was already dangerous because I knew anything at all. If anybody suspected what I knew, he wouldn't be able to help me. We both knew things could never be the same again. Frank said he wasn't going to spend all his shore leaves listening to sermons from me. Best thing I could do was get a place of my own by the time he got home again.'

There was no anger in Jeff's tone as he spoke of the scene with Frank. Rather, there was a hurt kind of sorrow.

'We parted more like deadly enemies than brothers. He had to go because of this other ship. I was confused and angry still. I thought

297

I'd have it out with Nielson and the others.'

'You really were confused,' I said. 'You heard what Frank had said about those guys.'

'I heard him, yes. But it hadn't any real impact. Murder, that's from television, the movies. It's not for real, not for people like me. At least, it wasn't.'

He dropped his voice again. Susan gave him a little pat of encouragement.

'I followed Nielson out to the club again. I parked my car a good way from his and waited to see what he'd do. He didn't go to the club. He walked straight to my car and pushed a gun in my face. Said he'd seen me hanging around the house a few times lately, and now I was following him. Why? I wouldn't tell him anything. He took my wallet to see if I had any identification, and found enough in there to tell him I was Frank's brother. I wasn't especially afraid, even with the gun. I couldn't see he had any reason to kill me. He said he couldn't waste any more time on me, because he had an appointment. He tied my hands to the wheel with his tie, then went to his own car for some rope. When he got back he roped me up completely, then shoved a handkerchief in my mouth to stop me yelling. Once he was satisfied I'd keep a while he told me he'd be back to continue our interesting talk. Did Frank ever tell you I get crazes?'

The question seemed out of place. Puzzled, I nodded.

'Yes. He said you couldn't seem to get your mind set on one thing. Why?'

'May have saved my life that time. You know what I had a big whirl at, a couple of years ago? Escapology. You know, the Houdini bit. I was out of that rope in less than five minutes. I knew I hadn't much time, and Nielson would be back any minute, but I had to do something positive. So I took the distributor head off his motor, and hid. He came out running in a stumbling kind of way, got in the car and of course it wouldn't start. Then he did a funny thing, or it seemed funny at the time. He went to this big Packard, got in and drove off. He didn't even bother about me. When I saw he wasn't heading back to town I thought I'd follow him again. The rest you know.'

I thought about it for a minute or two.

'You mean I know about the crash,' I corrected. 'Why should the police think it was you in the Packard?'

'As I told you, Nielson had taken my wallet. There was plenty of evidence there to say he was Jeff Hawkins.'

'Sure,' I agreed. 'But you knew you weren't dead. Why didn't you correct them?'

He rubbed a hand over his face.

'I'd had it,' he replied. 'My brother was a crook, and he'd told me to be missing when he came home. I didn't know whether Nielson might have told those others about me, the Elmans and Mrs Augustin. If he had, I might be in real trouble. It seemed like an opportunity from heaven and I'd be a fool to turn it down. I hadn't any family to worry about, no real friends.'

'Except Susan,' I pointed out.

'Naturally, except Susan. I meant to get in touch with Frank later just to let him know I was O.K. I couldn't go too far away, because of Sue, so I just came out here and buried myself. It wasn't difficult. What are you going to do about it?'

'Me?' I asked in surprise. 'Why should I do anything about it? It doesn't seem to be any of my business.'

Susan looked at me gratefully. Jeff wasn't so sure.

'You mean it? You're not going to sell this to some newspaper or something like that?'

I shook my head.

'I have my own ways of turning a dollar. That isn't one of them. Oh, and talking of dollars.'

I took out a brown envelope and laid it on

300

the table in front of him.

'What's that?'

'We call it money,' I explained. 'There's seven hundred dollars there. Frank had it in his pocket when he died. That makes it yours.'

He wagged his head and looked stubborn.

'No it doesn't. That's dirty money and I don't want it.'

I sighed and took out a slip of paper from the envelope.

'I thought you might give me an argument. That's a pay statement from the shipping company. The name on it is Frank Hawkins, and the amount due is just under eight hundred dollars. That money was earned in an honest profession. Now take it.'

He picked up the slip and read it carefully. Susan watched, but made no attempt to interfere. Then he said,

'O.K, and thanks, Mr Preston.'

It was over. I got up and we shook hands. Susan kissed me quickly and shyly on the cheek. She made me feel a hundred and ten years old. I left them sitting there and drove slowly back towards town. The first time I saw a call-box I swung in and started looking for change.

'It's Preston,' I announced, when I was connected.

Julie Van Dorn said,

'Well, well. I've been reading about you in the newspapers. I would have thought I was entitled to a first-hand report. Where are you?'

'On my way back to town. I've been clearing up odds and ends.'

'With a woman, I'll bet,' she accused.

'She'll be a woman in another few years,' I agreed. 'Know what she did? She kissed me on the cheek. I felt a hundred and ten years old.'

Julie chuckled with rich amusement.

'She must be very young. You need somebody older. I could make you feel a hundred and fifty without really trying.'

'I'll be there in thirty minutes,' I promised.